THE WIDOW'S CRUISE

by Nicholas Blake

A Nigel Strangeways Mystery

"A murder-shadowed cruise among Grecian isles, seen through the shrewd eyes of Nigel Strangeways and enriched by Blake's characteristic combination of equally firm novel-writing and crime-plotting."
—Anthony Boucher,
New York Times Book Review

"Lively and literate, with good scenery."
—Sergeant Cuff,
Saturday Review

"Nicholas Blake is one of the best in the business, should never be missed."
—*Boston Globe*

Other titles by Nicholas Blake
available in Perennial Library:

Nicholas Blake

The Widow's Cruise

PERENNIAL LIBRARY
Harper & Row, Publishers
New York, Hagerstown, San Francisco, London

Designed by Eve Callahan

First PERENNIAL LIBRARY edition published 1977

ISBN:0−06−080399−1

81 10 9 8 7 6 5

For Peter and Louise

" ''Tis double death to drown in ken of shore."

SHAKESPEARE

Contents

Prologue

THERE WAS SOMETHING wrong with the swans that May afternoon. A chilly, tetchy wind rasped over the Serpentine, ruffling their feathers and unsettling, it seemed, their nerves. They could not keep still. A swan rose heraldically upright, splatting the water with cumbrous, half-arm blows, then tore unprovoked at a companion which had been gloomily surveying its reflection, and chased it out of sight beyond the bridge. Another swan, in a state of manic exasperation, kept pecking viciously at something under its lifted wing—an action which caused it to career and flounder, feathers disorganized, neck like a snake striking. Several other swans, as if swept by mass hysteria, began to dig themselves furiously in the ribs.

"Do you suppose they have ants in their armpits?" asked Clare.

"I think they're having a nervous breakdown," Nigel replied.

"Well, if they are, they're overdoing it badly."

"Or it could be a form of neuromimesis."

"Whatever it is, it's extremely undignified," said Clare Massinger severely.

"You can't expect even a swan to be dignified when it's got an itch. I don't suppose Zeus looked very dignified when he was assaulting Leda."

"That was different."

A swan plodded from the Serpentine onto dry land, stretching out its neck for a piece of bread proffered by a nursemaid.

"It looks like an Edwardian hat trying to walk," remarked Clare. Her long, blue-black hair swirled like smoke in a gust of wind, and turning away she found herself confronting the Peter Pan statue, which she contemplated in silence for a period of time.

"You know," she said at last, "it has a lack of fascination all its own."

As they walked away arm in arm toward Lancaster Gate, Clare reverted to the queer manifestation they had just witnessed.

"Don't you think we ought to do something about them, darling?"

"The swans? What?"

"Well, ring somebody up and tell them the birds are verminous or demented or whatever it is. Who's responsible for them?"

"Oh, the Board of Works, I dare say; or the L.C.C. I've no idea. But that's reminded me. I rang up Swan's this morning. All their Hellenic cruises are booked up for this year. I've put our names down, in case any of the passengers cry off. But I think we ought to try for one of this new series of cruises Michael was talking about. It'd mean starting from Athens instead of Venice; but we could have a few days in Athens first, by ourselves."

Clare Massinger had recently come to that point, which

nearly every artist experiences two or three times in a working life, when the reservoir seems empty and some radical change of style or content necessary if the work is not to become a meaningless repetition of past achievement. In Greece, she felt, she might refresh her vision as a sculptor and recharge her batteries. Since neither she nor Nigel could speak the language, some sort of conducted tour would be the best way to get what she needed, in the limited time they had at their disposal.

She agreed now that they should inquire about the cruises which had just been started by the Prytanis line. Nigel Strangeways visited the Greek Tourist Office next morning. There were berths available on the S.S. *Menelaos*, he was told, sailing from Athens on September 1. The ship would visit Delos and then a number of islands in the Dodecanese, returning to the mainland by way of Crete, with expeditions to Epidaurus, Mycenae, and Delphi. The passengers would be mainly British and American, but there was a small party of French also, and a sprinkling of Germans and Italians. There were to be Greek guides on board, and several lecturers of European reputation, including a distinguished Byzantine scholar, the Bishop of Solway, and that famous Hellenophile and popularizer of classical Greek literature, Jeremy Street.

Nigel had no hesitation in booking passages. The itinerary of the *Menelaos*, taking in so many islands whose very names had the ring of legend, sounded altogether admirable. Clare's dark eyes lit up when he told her where they would be going. Nigel felt no premonition that this itinerary would carry him into a labyrinth of human motives darker and more complex than the dwelling of the Minotaur.

Embarkation

SIXTEEN WEEKS LATER, Nigel was leaning on the rail of the promenade deck, looking at the shipping in the Piraeus. This morning he and Clare had paid a last visit to the Theater of Dionysus and the Acropolis. The heat—it was nearly 100 degrees in the shade—and the perfect majesty of the Parthenon had silenced them. Even Clare's inordinate appetite for sight-seeing was temporarily sated; so, after a leisurely lunch, they took a taxi to the Piraeus, with the view of settling in before the mass of passengers arrived.

The *Menelaos* had been lying at the quayside for thirty-six hours and the cabins were suffocatingly hot. Opening the porthole of Clare's, which adjoined his own on the main deck, was enough to bring Nigel out in a profuse sweat. Clare announced that she was going to have a strip-wash, and then "get everything ship-shape"—a procedure which would involve, Nigel had no doubt, unpacking and strewing her clothes all over her own bunk and that of her fellow-occupant, a Miss E. Jamieson, B.A., who had fortunately not yet turned up. Nigel left her to it, fought his way through a blast of heat to open the porthole of his own cabin, which, the passenger list told him, he would be sharing with Dr. Stephen Plunket, M.D., M.Sc., neatly disposed his belongings, and came out on deck gasping for air. Having filled in time investigating the main features of the vessel—the two saloons, forward and aft, the bars (not open yet), the small swimming pool (still dry) on the forecastle beneath the bridge—Nigel took up his position at the port rail of the promenade deck amidships.

Beneath him, a flat tanker was oiling the *Menelaos* through an umbilical cord of pipeline. Beyond, the blue and white flags of three Greek corvettes, moored together, rippled in a light breeze that had risen. There were three passenger vessels, their white paint dazzling in the Athenian sunlight, lying stem to stern at the quays opposite; one of these, the S.S. *Adriatici,* was the ship chartered by Swan's on which Nigel had unsuccessfully tried to get berths for Clare and himself. A large P. & O. cruise liner, with a single funnel like a huge yellow pepper pot, was getting up steam. Some weather-beaten tramp steamers, a gaggle of assorted small craft, warehouses, ship cranes and the hazy blue-white sky made up the rest of the scene. In the air hung a pervasive smell—fumes from the tanker mingled with an odor of, was it Greek cooking, or decaying vegetables, or both? It might be convenient, thought Nigel, that he was sharing a cabin with the ship's doctor.

Nigel tried to imagine this place in the fifth century, with the triremes coming in and the Long Walls running up to Athens; but the heat had taken all the spring out of his imagination. A sudden outburst of sound, from the other side of the *Menelaos,* broke into his thoughts. Moving over to the starboard side and looking down on the quay to which the ship was moored, Nigel saw a truck laden with rectangular chunks of ice. A sailor, standing on a makeshift cradle hung from the deck, was passing these into the ship through a porthole, one by one, as they were handed up to him. A violent altercation had blown up between the overseer of the shore party handling the ice and a ship's officer who was leaning over the rail twenty feet away from Nigel. Whether the ice had arrived late, or was the wrong shape, or whether the two disputants just disliked each other's faces, Nigel had no means of determining. But the scene could not have been more dramatic if it had been leading up to the crisis of an ancestral blood feud. At one point the ship's officer actually tore his hair in despair—a gesture Nigel had not witnessed since attending an Q.U.D.S. performance of *Oedipus* thirty years ago. What most impressed him, though, was the rhythm of the exchanges. The officer shouted, in the staccato, stabbing language of his nation, accompanying the speech with a wealth of murderous gesture, while the overseer stood listening. Then the overseer screamed back, dancing hysterically on his feet as though at any moment he might rise into the air and strangle the officer, while the latter heard him out, chewing his brigand-like mustache. Strophe and antistrophe, thought Nigel; the noble Athenian tradition of argument—of listening to your opponent's case as well as voicing your own. It was this sort of thing, Nigel realized, which made your heart warm to the Greeks—made you love them, passionately, indiscriminately, and forever.

"Is blood going to flow?" came the light, high voice of Clare beside him.

"Oh, you're here. No, they're just having a little difference of opinion about ice."

The combatants shrieked at each other, alternately, for a few minutes longer. Then, as abruptly as it had blown up, the storm ended. The overseer spat at the virgin-white side of the ship; the officer made a gesture which might have expressed the whole tragedy of King Lear, and turned away. Honor was satisfied, emotion exhausted.

On the quay below, emerging from buses and taxis, passengers were now beginning to arrive. They had to run the gantlet of a horde of hucksters, selling everything from Greek vases (twentieth century) to lemonade, from hunks of pink melon to Evzone dolls. Nigel and Clare played the time-honored travelers' game of speculating about the characters, professions, and provenance of these still unknown fellow-travelers. They had just spotted a Royal Academician (who later proved to be the Bishop of Solway) and a trio of classical schoolmasters (who turned out to be, respectively, an analytical chemist, a barrister, and a civil servant), when their attention was drawn by two women strolling slowly toward the gangway. Or, rather, by one of them. Of middle height, her graceful carriage minimizing a certain stockiness of figure, with high cheekbones and charming hollows beneath them, and a delicate brown complexion that, when she came closer, showed itself as a triumph of cosmetic art, this woman had that air of sexual awareness which tells its own story. She wore a lemon-colored linen suit and a wide white straw hat.

"Oh look!" said Clare. "Here comes the ship's *femme fatale.*"

The woman's companion, though of the same height, seemed dumpy in comparison. She wore a puce-colored jumper which emphasized the muddiness of her skin, a rumpled tweed skirt, and serviceable shoes. The general effect of a badly done-up parcel was heightened by untidy hair, a shambling gait, and restless, spasmodic gestures. As she looked up at the ship, her mouth jerked uncontrollably, and she put up a hand as if to hold it still. It was at this moment that Nigel heard a girl, standing at the rail beside him, exclaim:

"Oh God! Peter, look! There's the Bross. What on earth is she doing here?"

"The Bross?"

"Miss Ambrose. You know."

There was such dismay in the girl's voice that Nigel looked up sharply. The girl had gone white; her thin body was hunched, almost as if she expected a blow, and her hands were clenched on the rail. She was sixteen or seventeen, Nigel judged, and the boy with her was obviously her brother—a twin brother, very likely.

"Don't worry, Faith," he said, taking her arm. "She's seeing somebody off, I expect."

"It'll spoil everything if—"

"Don't be a goat. She can't eat you."

"Look, she's coming up the gangway." The girl ducked her head—a queer, involuntary movement—then hurried away down the deck, her brother following her with a grim look on his face which Nigel was to remember.

The oddly assorted couple were now climbing the gangway. As she handed in her embarkation card, the beauty threw the purser a dazzling, slightly lopsided smile which gave character to her exquisitely made-up face. Her companion, eyes averted, shuffled past, and the pair went off toward their cabin, followed by stewards carrying their luggage.

"Well, what do you make of them? A rich divorcée traveling with her secretary?"

"They're sisters," said Clare firmly.

"*Sisters?* Oh, nonsense!"

"Yes. Identical bone structure. One's a successful *mondaine,* the other a neurotic. That's what put you off. I look at the skull beneath the skin."

"You should know. One of them is Miss Ambrose, anyway; a schoolmistress, probably, judging by our young friend's consternation just now. That'd be the sallow, twitching one. Let's look at the passenger list."

This document, which had been handed to them on embarking, showed that Cabin 3 on A deck was to be occupied by Mrs. Melissa Blaydon and Miss Ianthe Ambrose.

"Well, they may be sisters," said Nigel. "Those elegant, classical Christian names suggest one father. But I still think it's perverse of the expensive Melissa to be holidaying with a string bag like Ianthe."

"Perversity makes strange bedfellows."

"Ambrose. Ambrose. I wonder could it be E. K. Ambrose?"

"Who's he?"

"He was a very distinguished Greek scholar. Did definitive editions of Euripides. I read them at Oxford."

II

During the several hours that elapsed before dinner, the passengers began to sort themselves out. National characteristics were soon in evidence. The blond individuals, slung around with cameras, haversacks, and guidebooks, who marched purposefully up and down the boat deck, could only be Germans. The French contingent, who had brought their own lecturer, gravitated together at one end of the forward saloon, where they chattered incessantly, ignoring their fellow-travelers. A few Italian men, dressed in flashy lounge suits, strolled about the ship escorting their wives and regarding with brilliant admiration every other personable female in sight. The Americans waited for the bars to open; while the British tried to avoid one another, glancing in a furtive and resentful manner at anyone they suspected of a tendency to interrupt their interminable postcard writing.

There were exceptions of course. A fat-faced man got into conversation with Nigel and Clare, introducing himself as Ivor Bentinck-Jones. He was no stranger in these parts, he told them, and if they wanted to know the ropes, he was their man. With his twinkling eyes, jolly voice, and evidently unsnubbable nature, Mr. Bentinck-Jones was cut out to be the life and soul of the ship. His eagerness to make friends, though a little pathetic, was not unlikable. He seemed the sort of man, thought Nigel, who would attract confidences as a beggar attracts charity.

"Are you quite satisfied with your cabin?" the man presently asked. "If not, Nikki would change it for you, I'm sure. He's the cruise manager, you know."

"Our cabins are quite comfortable, thank you," replied Clare.

"Oh, I see. Good. Sorry—I thought you were traveling together."

"So we are."

A momentarily discouraged look came into the man's eye. Clare felt quite bad at depriving him of the mild pleasure he would have derived from meeting a couple living in sin on shipboard. "We are just good friends," she satirically added.

"Hello, there's Jeremy Street." Ivor Bentinck-Jones waved at a man who was approaching—a tall, distinguished figure, with a young-old face, thinning golden hair, and the consciously unobtrusive manner of a celebrity who knows his own market value and does not need to assert it. Jeremy Street wore an immaculate white linen suit, a royal-blue shirt, and a silk neckerchief, the ensemble giving him the appearance of one of those would-be U types to be found in a Harrod's catalogue.

"Met him on the train," confided Bentinck-Jones. "Delightful fellow. No side at all. . . . Ah, Street, let me introduce you. Mr. Jeremy Street. Miss Clare Massinger. Mr. Nigel Strangeways."

The three murmured politely at one another.

"It's a great pleasure to meet you," said the newcomer to Clare. "I saw your last exhibition. Such strength and delicacy. That Madonna particularly. The earthy touched with the divine—as it should be."

Jeremy Street's voice was almost too melodious, his respectful yet manly tone almost too perfectly suitable. A faint qualm of distaste, perceptible only to Nigel, came and went on Clare's face.

"Hello, hello, hello," caroled Ivor Bentinck-Jones. "Another celebrity on board. You're a painter, Miss Massinger?"

"Sculptor."

"Well, you've come to the fountainhead of European art," he proclaimed.

"So I'm told," said Clare.

" 'The isles of Greece, the isles of Greece, where burning

Sappho loved and sung,' " continued Mr. Bentinck-Jones, his pudgy face convulsed with enthusiasm. "What inspiration! But it is not your first visit, I am sure."

"Yes. My first visit."

"Well, well. And under what better auspices than those of the renowned Jeremy Street?"

The renowned Jeremy Street glanced apologetically at Clare, his mobile mouth twitching at one corner. There was a limit, perhaps, to his capacity for being lionized.

"And may we expect another translation from your pen in the near future?" inquired Mr. Bentinck-Jones.

"I've just finished the *Hippolytus.*"

"Ah. One of Sophocles' most noble works."

"Euripides, actually."

"Euripides, of course. What an absurd slip of the tongue."

Nigel asked, "What text have you used? E. K. Ambrose, I suppose."

The question could hardly have been more innocuous. But Nigel was instantly aware that, somehow, it had given offense. The wrinkled, young-old face went tight, with a huffy, defensive look.

"Ambrose was very sound," he said, "but somewhat lacking in imaginative sympathy. One wonders sometimes if these classical academics have the faintest idea what goes on in a poet's mind."

"There's an Ianthe Ambrose on board," said Nigel. "I wonder if—"

"What? I.A.?" The words seemed to explode out of Jeremy Street before he could check them.

"You know her?"

"Not personally," answered the lecturer with repressive hauteur, and shortly bade them *au revoir.*

Nigel was left with two impressions: that the unfortunate Ianthe Ambrose must have the gift of making enemies; and that Ivor Bentinck-Jones had not merely sensed Jeremy Street's discomposure at her presence on board, but had abscurely relished it. No doubt, as with most busybodies, there was a streak of malice in his make-up.

"I suspect they're both phonies," Clare was murmuring.

"Phonies? Who?"

"Our Jeremy and our Ivor. Jeremy is vain as a peacock but probably harmless. Ivor, on the other hand—"

"Well? What's wrong with him?"

"He thought the *Hippolytus* was written by Sophocles. And did you notice how he was pumping us? If we knew what was going on behind that jolly façade, I'm not at all sure we should like it. And his eyes are too small."

Whatever Mr. Bentinck-Jones's propensities might be, Jeremy Street was soon to appear in an unexpected light. Clare had gone below to fetch her sketching block, and Nigel was strolling along the promenade deck. As he passed a window of the reading room, which adjoined the B saloon aft, his eye was caught by a figure within. It was Jeremy Street. Something warily insouciant in his pose reminded Nigel of a shoplifter he had once spotted in the act. Street's back was turned to the window; his hand went out to a beige-covered magazine which lay on the table before him and whipped it inside his coat. That beige cover was not unfamiliar to Nigel. Why, he wondered as he moved on, should a distinguished lecturer on classical subjects possess himself, in so guilty a fashion, of the *Journal of Classical Studies?* There seemed to be only one answer; unless the man was a straight kleptomaniac, he had taken the *Journal* away from the reading room to prevent fellow-passengers reading it. An ineffective precaution surely, though, for on a cruise of this sort it was pretty certain that some passengers would have brought copies of their own. Nigel made a mental note to procure a copy of the quarterly; he had already formed a theory as to why Jeremy Street should have abstracted it, but he liked verifying his conjectures.

III

Dinner in the A saloon was nearly over. Nigel and Clare had been assigned to a table whose other occupants were the Bishop of Solway and his wife, Mrs. Hale. The Bishop's white vandyke beard, which had made them mistake him for an R.A., wagged as vigorously over his food as his wife's tongue wagged over their fellow-passengers. Already, in a few hours, she had somehow accumulated several dossiers; and where her actual knowledge was deficient, her imagination readily filled the gaps.

"My dear Tilly," her husband had protested at one point, "Miss Massinger will think you're a terrible gossip."

"I never gossip, Edwin. I am gossiped *to*. It all comes of looking so fat and comfy and normal. I'm a Mum figure—everyone coughs it up in my lap."

"Little do they know your real nature," remarked the Bishop darkly.

Mrs. Hale did indeed resemble a vivacious roly-poly at first sight; but there was a smoldering, sardonic glint in her eyes which should have warned the unwary.

"Have you met Beauty and the Beast yet?" she asked, glancing across to the table where Mrs. Blaydon and Miss Ambrose sat.

"No," said Clare. "They are sisters, aren't they?"

"Yes. Miss Ambrose is a schoolteacher—classics. She's had a nervous breakdown and her sister has brought her on this cruise to convalesce. I would think it'd rather cramp Mrs. Blaydon's style, having the woman around all the time."

"Cramp her style?" inquired Nigel.

"Melissa Blaydon is the Merry Widow *de nos jours*—"

"Actually a widow?"

"Yes. And it's quite apparent to me that she has only one interest in life. Men. They've started to swarm around her already. But Ianthe Ambrose positively growls and bares her teeth at them. I can't see Mrs. Blaydon getting much shipboard romance."

"My dear Tilly," remarked the Bishop. "Only a contortionist could commit misconduct in these packing cases they call cabins here, anyway."

"My husband does not talk like this at diocesan conferences," his wife reassured them.

The Bishop of Solway gave a sharp bark of laughter, his blue eyes twinkling. "You've no idea how I talk at diocesan conferences." He beamed at his wife with great affection.

"How do you know all this about Mrs. Blaydon?" Clare asked.

"She happened to be sitting next to me on the boat deck before dinner, and a podgy little man called Bentinck-Jones got into conversation with her."

"Ah ha," said Clare. "She told him about her sister? He's got a quite insatiable curiosity about other people's lives, I suspect. You'd better watch out."

"Oh, my life's an open book," Mrs. Hale declared.

"An open book," said her husband, "filled with improper pictures. You would hardly credit how luxuriant an imagination my wife has, Miss Massinger. It comes of the humdrum life she has to lead with me in the Palace." He patted his bearded mouth with his napkin, and glanced mischievously at his wife. "Their father and I were Fellows of the same college in the old days. There's nothing I can't tell you about the Ambrose sisters, when they were children."

"Well, really, Edwin! Why have you been keeping this from us?"

The Bishop's expression changed. "It's rather a sad story. I don't intend to rake it up, even for you, Tilly."

"They remind me of a poem by Edwin Muir," said Nigel, after a pause; he had been covertly eying the sisters. "It's about two creatures, inveterate enemies, which have to fight each other, over and over again. One is 'the crested animal in its pride, arrayed in all the royal hues.' The other is—how does it go?—'a soft round beast as brown as clay' —'a battered bag he might have been.' Muir dreamed about them, I believe, while he was being psychoanalyzed."

"And which won?" the Bishop's wife asked.

"The beautiful crested animal always wins, but it can never kill its enemy."

A queer little silence came over their table. Nigel was conscious of the Bishop's eyes upon him.

"You're right about one thing," said the latter at last. But what Nigel was right about did not emerge, for at this moment a loud, metallic voice silenced all conversation in the saloon.

At the far end, a man was speaking through a microphone.

"My name is Nikolaides. I am your cruise manager. Welcome, ladies and gentlemen, to Greece and the *Menelaos*. I hope you shall all have a mighty fine cruise."

The man paused to distribute dazzling smiles to the customers, and Mrs. Hale was heard to mutter, "The Billy Butlin of the Aegean. He'll be calling us 'lads and lasses' any moment."

Mr. Nikolaides resumed, speaking fluently in an American accent. He told them where his office was, announced the plans for tomorrow's expedition at Delos, urged them to bring any complaints to him personally, and begged them all to call him Nikki.

He was a broad-shouldered man of medium height, with a swarthy, clean-shaven face, flashing white teeth, black oiled hair that shone like a tarmac road after rain, and a personality whose magnetism could be felt the whole length of the saloon.

"And now," he concluded, "has anyone any questions to ask me?"

"Yes. What time is this ship actually going to start?" The questioner was, of all people, Ianthe Ambrose. Her voice was slurred, deepish, peremptory; and, though the question was not in itself offensive, she contrived to make it sound thoroughly disagreeable. The tension in the woman communicated itself to all the diners, who shifted uncomfortably in their chairs, avoiding one another's eyes. Only Nikki seemed unaffected.

"In a couple of hours' time," he said. "We are delayed because the oil tanker arrived late. But do not worry. We shall catch up with our schedule O.K."

He walked now from table to table, greeting the passengers individually. At the table where Melissa and Ianthe sat, he paused rather longer; he spoke reassuringly to the latter, but while he did so his eyes kept returning to her sister. One can almost see a spark in the air where their glances meet, thought Nigel. Melissa Blaydon's profile, set off by the Indian headscarf she wore, was ravishing in its purity of line. The little tableau was broken up by a movement of Ianthe's hand—an abrupt, seemingly involuntary movement which knocked over a wineglass. Nikki snapped his fingers, a steward hurried to the table, Ianthe's sallow face darkened unbecomingly.

When he came over to their own table, Nikki greeted the Bishop of Solway and his wife respectfully, then bowed over Clare's hand, his eyes alight with a frank, almost animal admiration. There was an innocence about it, a sort of pagan *joie de vivre* in his whole face, which disarmed one; and, though his manner was deferential, it lacked any trace of obsequiousness.

"What nice eyes he has," said Clare when Nikki had moved away. "Like prunes soaked in electricity."

The Bishop gave his sharp grunt of laughter.

Mrs. Hale said, "A bull. A shining bull. He was almost pawing the ground."

"Well, as long as he doesn't paw me," Clare murmured.

"Extraordinary—how the Greeks have kept their old tradition of independence," said the Bishop. "Poor but proud. Look at the stewards. Not like waiters at all. Free men. It's in their bearing, and stamped on their faces."

"Something to do with the austere way of life they have to live?" suggested Nigel. "It makes for simplicity, for staying unspoiled. Nikki, for instance; he's built on simple lines, I'd say, like a Homeric hero."

"I don't much like their Homeric coffee," said Mrs. Hale, sipping distastefully. "Whatever can it be made of?"

"Grumble, grumble, grumble," her husband remarked.

IV

They were sitting on the afterdeck, under the arc lights and the stars. From a café beyond the quays, a loud-speaker bellowed dance music, drowning the murmur of conversation all around them. Passengers sauntered up and down, or leaned over the rail, waiting for the ship to start.

Clare put her hand on Nigel's, sighing. "I'm glad we're here, darling."

"Yes."

"And I like the Bish and Mrs. They're a good advertisement for marriage."

"We're lucky to have them for table-mates. Have you come across your cabin companion yet?"

"Yes. Quite harmless. She teaches Greek somewhere— some university. She's brought quite a library of books and magazines with her. Funny, coming to Greece to read."

"Well, you might borrow the current number of the *Journal of Classical Studies* from her, if she has it. Don't forget."

"All right. Why?"

"I could fancy a read of it at breakfast tomorrow. Hello, who's this?"

A small girl—she might have been ten years old—had drifted along the deck and come to anchor opposite them. Her fattish, shapeless body struck Nigel as being a replica, in miniature, of Ianthe Ambrose's. She wore an embroidered blouse and a serge skirt, over which hung what appeared to be a sporran. She had a notebook in her hand as she stood there, regarding them expressionlessly through thick-glassed spectacles.

"Well, and who are you?" asked Nigel.

The child advanced till she was all but standing on Nigel's feet, before replying, in a clear, pedantic tone, "My name is Primrose Chalmers. Who are you?"

"I am Nigel Strangeways, and this is Clare Massinger."

The child paused to record the information in her notebook.

"Are you married?" she then inquired.

"No."

"Living together?"

Nigel reached out and pretended to snip off the child's nose between first and second fingers.

"Castration symbolism, that is," the child bleakly announced.

Nigel withdrew his hand as if he had been stung. Clare giggled.

"What on earth do you know about——?"

"My father and mother are lay analysts," said Primrose Chalmers.

"Well, isn't that nice!" Clare remarked. "Are they traveling with you?"

"Yes. I have been in analysis myself for seven years."

"I'm not surpr—" Clare bit it off. "That's a long time. You must be madly normal by now. And here you are in Greece, at the source of the Oedipus complex."

Primrose scowled at her, and made an entry in the notebook.

"Hey, hey! There's a chiel amang us taking notes," came the voice of Mr. Bentinck-Jones from nearby.

"What do you write in your book?" asked Nigel.

"I am compiling data about the passengers, with a view to an essay on group psychology," the formidable child answered.

"Crikey! Don't you ever take a holiday?"

Primrose deemed this question unworthy of reply. Turning to Ivor Bentinck-Jones, she began the questionnaire.

"I think, if you're going to Gallup poll me, young lady," he said with a wink at Nigel, "it had better be done in private."

"It's not a Gallup poll," Primrose severely corrected him. But, putting away notebook and fountain pen in her sporran, she walked off with the obliging Bentinck-Jones.

"Well, what next? Poor wretched child."

"Two children," said Clare, surveying the retreating backs of Ivor and Primrose. "A couple of inquisitive children. They'll get on famously."

"That's what worries me. Shan't be long, love." Nigel pulled himself out of his deck chair and sauntered slowly after the figures of Primrose Chalmers and Ivor Bentinck-Jones. Nigel's passionate curiosity about human beings was accompanied by a deep distrust of persons who, outside their professional capacities, manifested the same curiosity. Experience had taught him that such curiosity is seldom disinterested. Bentinck-Jones, for instance; he might just be the fulsome, pathetic lonely heart he appeared to be; or a genuine child-lover whose heart was big enough to include even the rebarbative Primrose. Or again, he might not.

At a respectful distance, Nigel followed the pair along the portside of the boat deck. They climbed a ladder up to the bridge deck. When Nigel arrived there, they had disappeared. On his left was a row of deck houses, the quarters of the *Menelaos'* officers. He passed between them and a ship's boat into an open space of deck forward of the bridge and beneath it, and walked around to the starboard side. Here too a single ship's boat was accommodated. Passengers were sitting or strolling here, but not the two he had followed. Perhaps they had gone into the radio room, aft of the Captain's cabin. Nigel peered in. The room was empty. They must have gone up the portside ladder only to descend the starboard one. But then, why should Bentinck-Jones have brought Primrose up here at all?

Nigel had reached the head of the starboard ladder again when he heard a low voice. Bentinck-Jones's. It came from the far side of the ship's boat. The man must have found a space between the boat and the rail, where he and Primrose could have a private confabulation. He was speaking in a whisper now, so that Nigel missed a good deal of what he was saying. But what Nigel did hear was sufficiently intriguing.

". . . you can help me. I'm in the Secret Service. . . . Two EOKA agents on board—don't know which of the passengers . . . might be a woman. . . . Nobody would suspect you. . . . Keep your eyes and ears open . . . anything anyone says or does . . . suspicious . . . agents may try to make contact with. . . . Write it down in your notebook. . . . Anything that strikes you as odd, in the way people behave or . . . you never know what . . . pieces of jigsaw puzzle. Got the idea?"

"Yes. I see." Primrose sounded excited, as well she might. "And I'm to tell you—"

"Ssh! It's got to be a deadly secret between us. . . . I'll tell you when I . . . no dropping hints in public when we meet . . . anyone see your notebook. It's a bargain, then? Good girl. Cut along, then . . . mustn't be seen together too much."

Nigel moved smartly away. He was very thoughtful as he walked around beneath the bridge and descended the portside ladder to the boat deck. Ivor Bentinck-Jones's game might be just a game—something to amuse the child and take her mind off psychoanalysis. But there were less innocuous possibilities. One thing was certain—Secret Service agents did not reveal their profession to young schoolgirls. The man might, of course, be one of those harmless if tiresome characters who need grandiose fantasies to support their egos. Perhaps this Secret Service nonsense was a game he played seriously with himself.

Well, thought Nigel, time will show. Time did show, all too soon and all disastrously.

V

When Nigel returned to the afterdeck where he had left Clare he found the chairs beside her occupied by Mrs.

Blaydon and her sister. Clare introduced Nigel, and he sat down at her feet, saying:

"Primrose Chalmers has just been enrolled in the Secret Service."

"Now what can you mean by that?" asked Clare, without any pressing curiosity.

"It sounds like something in a game," said Mrs. Blaydon. "I hope it is."

Melissa Blaydon's long lashes fluttered at Nigel. She was clearly puzzled by this unconventional opening, and a little piqued that Nigel did not enlarge upon it. Her sister, sprawling lumpishly in the deck chair, seemed at first to be preoccupied with some inner argument; her greeny-brown eyes, which had not met Nigel's when they were introduced, stared at nothing in particular, her mouth twitched, and her fingers made little writhing movements in her lap. But, as the desultory conversation went on, Nigel began to get an impression that Ianthe Ambrose was not altogether bogged down in her own misery. Behind the collapsed façade, there was concealed an occupant both intelligent and attentive to what was going on. Once or twice she broke in with an incisive remark which showed her intelligence and had the effect of puncturing the subject. Her secret attentiveness, if it was not merely an effect of her inner tension, was more difficult to define; but Nigel presently got the feeling that it was directed against himself—that Ianthe Ambrose was playing the watchdog over her sister, ready to snap at any man who approached Melissa too close. Ianthe could simply be a man-hater; or there might be some more subtle source of jealousy involved.

Melissa herself he found rather a disappointment. Not that, at close quarters, her beauty was diminished; the curves and hollows of her animated face were exquisite, reminding him of Yeats's lines, "Did quattrocento finger fashion it Hollow of cheek as though it drank the wind And took a mess of shadows for its meat?" Her hands, too, were thin and graceful, though they might grow clawlike with the years. But Melissa Blaydon had very little, it seemed, inside that beautiful head. Her animation was artificial, her conversation that of a woman who has had her thinking done for her by others. It consisted largely in name-dropping and an enumeration of the places she had lived in and visited. Did they know Cannes well? Were not the shops in Rome absolute heaven? Capri had been ruined since Farouk went there. Greece, for Mrs. Blaydon, was chiefly distinguished as the birthplace of the Onassis brothers.

On the face of it, Melissa was no more than a spoiled, silly, selfish woman of the world. Yet, thought Nigel, she has taken time off from her futile life to bring this unprepossessing sister to a country in which she herself can have little interest. Natural sisterly affection? Guilt for past neglect? The latter, possibly; for it emerged in conversation that Mrs. Blaydon had been living in various places abroad ever since her marriage fifteen years ago.

"My sister has always wanted to visit Greece. She's the clever one of the family, you know. Father passed on all his brains to her."

A spasm of pain distorted Ianthe's face. She seemed about to blurt out something, but restrained herself.

"Your father was E. K. Ambrose?" said Nigel.

Melissa opened her eyes wide at him. "Oh, you knew him?"

"Only by reputation."

"My sister is following in his footsteps. I don't know why you haven't been asked to give some lectures on board, Ianthe."

"Oh, I couldn't compete with the great Jeremy Street."

"You don't approve of him?" ventured Nigel.

Ianthe's lifeless face suddenly sprang into animation, and for the first time Nigel saw that she and Melissa, as Clare had claimed, bore a close resemblance to each other beneath the surface.

"Approve of him? My dear man, Street is an absolute

charlatan. He picks other people's brains and then makes a mess of them. He simply has no conception of scholarship whatsoever."

As if this outburst had exhausted her, Miss Ambrose relapsed into apathy.

It was a few minutes later that Nigel observed approaching along the deck the blond girl who had taken fright when Ianthe Ambrose and her sister came up the gangway. Her brother was with her. On seeing Miss Ambrose now, she stopped dead, gripped her brother's arm, pulled him around, and began to walk away. A glance at Miss Ambrose told Nigel that she had not noticed this. The boy shook off his sister's hand. She disappeared from view; but the boy leaned with his back to the rail, fixedly gazing in the direction of Melissa and Ianthe. His face was in shadow. But Melissa Blaydon at once became conscious of his scrutiny.

"I'm going to have trouble with that young man," she announced in her deep, lazy voice.

"What young man?" asked Ianthe sharply.

"Over there. He keeps following me about and staring at me."

"Who is he?"

"I've no idea."

"His name is Peter," said Nigel. "And he has a sister called Faith."

"Faith what? Is she on board, do you mean?" Ianthe said, in her most peremptory voice.

"Yes. I don't know their surname. A blond girl, sixteen or seventeen. Rather pretty, but she has irregular teeth and a stoop."

As if aware that her last question had been extremely brusque, Ianthe spoke more forthcomingly. "Sounds as if it could be one of my ex-pupils. Faith Trubody. I seem to remember she has a twin brother. And why are you going to have trouble with him, Melissa?"

"He makes eyes at me. I seem to attract the young. It's

becoming quite a nuisance, at my age. Perhaps I'm fated to be a cradle-snatcher." She laughed, giving Nigel a rueful look. "You'll have to rescue me from him. The young do bore me so." There was a subtly caressive note in her voice, like a waft of some extremely delicate yet voluptuous perfume; and such was her sexual potency that, for a moment, the two other women sitting there might not have existed.

"Yes, here we are." Clare had consulted the passenger list. "Mr. Arthur Trubody, C.B.E., Peter Trubody, Faith Trubody. An ex-pupil, did you say she is?"

"Faith was not a very satisfactory girl, I'm afraid," Miss Ambrose replied, with a curious shake in her voice which was not lost on Nigel. "I'm very tired, Melissa. Are you going to stay up here all night?"

"Oh, don't let's go to bed yet. The air is so lovely and cool now—I'm sure it's good for us. You go if you like, though."

Ianthe Ambrose, however, made no move. Like a fog that had lifted only for a little, misery came down over her face again, shutting her out from the others.

"What school do you teach at, Miss Ambrose?" Clare presently asked. There was a silence, and Melissa had to reply.

"My sister was at Summerton till recently. She taught the top form classics. Just now, she's having a long rest before—"

"Oh, for God's sake, Mel, cut out the soothing syrup," her sister shockingly exclaimed. "I had a breakdown and they sacked me."

"I do think it was absolutely iniquitous of them," said Melissa. "After all, it wasn't as if—" Her voice trailed away helplessly, and she gave an ugly little shrug of the shoulders.

"Well, ladies, everything to your liking, I hope? You care for a pillow, Mrs. Blaydon?" Nikki had come up, radiating charm and good will, his broad shoulders blocking out a considerable segment of the night sky.

"Yes, thank you, Mr. Nikolaides," said Melissa.

"Ah now, I hope we shall not stand on ceremony. Everyone calls me Nikki. Say, you are all English, yes? I love particularly the English."

"All of them, Nikki?" Melissa Blaydon's tone was decidedly flirtatious.

"Sure thing! All of them. A great people. And the English women are the most beautiful in the world." Nikki made an expansive gesture.

"*All* of them?" Clare mischievously echoed.

"Two especially. Now, ladies, do not be offended. We Greeks are a simple people. When we admire, we say so. When we hate—" His teeth flashed at them like a man-eater's.

"But don't the Greeks hate us over Cyprus?"

"No, no, no, Mr. Strangeways. Your government is not popular with us. But we do not confuse people, individuals, with their government. We Greeks are great individualists."

The *Menelaos* came alive. Shouts were heard from the fo'c's'le and the quay. Nikki held up his finger.

"You hear? The engines are started. In a minute or two we are on our way."

"Mel, I'm not feeling good. I want to go below."

"Oh, Ianthe darling, wouldn't you like just to watch us steaming out of harbor? It's always so exciting."

Ianthe's voice, which had been low and urgent, now rose to a kind of muffled shriek.

"I can't stand it when the siren goes!"

"Darling, there's no siren here."

"That thing on the funnel. The steam whistle. We're so near it. My nerves won't stand it, I tell you! It'll be going off any minute now! Please, please, pl—"

"All right, dearest. Come along, then. Good night, everyone."

Melissa's arm around Ianthe's waist, the two sisters hurried away. Nikki stared after them, then sauntered off along the deck.

"Well!" said Clare. "That poor thing ought to be in a

nursing home still. I do hope we're not going to have trouble with her, on the voyage."

"Anyway, she managed to detach Melissa from the magnetic Nikki."

"Oh, Nigel, you don't think—?"

"I think she's going to be a proper ball and chain for Melissa, one way or another."

"I rather like Melissa."

"She's a nitwit. But she seems to have a heart."

The steam whistle gave a long, groaning bellow. Passengers, jumping up from their chairs, crowded to the rail. The screws began to thrash, and, almost imperceptibly at first, the *Menelaos* edged away from the quayside.

Fraternization

NIGEL STRANGEWAYS awoke early next morning, roused by the sunlight streaming through the porthole onto the upper bunk, which he occupied. Lowering himself cautiously to the floor, so as not to disturb his cabin companion, Dr. Plunket, he put on bathing trunks, took a towel, and sought the swimming pool on the fo'c's'le.

It had been filled during the night, and sailors were now rigging an awning above it, which extended to shelter several feet of deck on either side of the pool itself. Walking to the bows, Nigel looked about him. Astern, just visible still, lay an island which, if the *Menelaos* had caught up with her schedule, should be Siros, the capital of the Cyclades. The sun, climbing on his left hand, was already giving off enough heat to warm the deck beneath his bare feet. On the starboard beam a caique rose and dipped on the waves, and two tawny-colored sea birds, flying low, escorted the *Menelaos,* crisscrossing her bows. Dead ahead, a small low island, rising at one point to a hill, must be Delos, with Mount Kynthos crowning it. A bar of pure turquoise color, some effect of sun and shallows, reached out from the island at a diagonal, contrasting with the royal blue of the sea on this side and the pale green beyond.

The sailors finished putting up the awning and retired, chattering among themselves like grasshoppers. Looking aft from the bows, Nigel saw, over the top of the awning, the windows of the forward lounge, and above them the bridge, on one wing of which stood a ship's officer, and the wheelhouse.

He plunged into the swimming pool. The water was deliciously cold. There was only space to swim half a dozen strokes, but it had a good depth—with his toes on the bottom, the water came up to Nigel's chin, and he was six feet tall.

After thrashing around for a while, he was about to get out when Primrose Chalmers appeared. She was still wearing the blouse, the serge skirt, and the sporran—indeed, they looked as if she had slept in them; but these were now topped by a Venetian gondolier's straw hat with a green ribbon dangling down behind.

"Is it deep?" the child asked.

"About five feet, six inches. Can you swim?"

"Yes. But I prefer the sea. Swimming baths are full of bacilli."

Nigel shuddered and got out smartly, sitting down on the low parapet of the pool.

"How's the play therapy going?" he asked.

"Play therapy? Isn't that something the psychiatrists make you do?" Primrose uttered the word "psychiatrists" with all the contempt of the Freudian analyst.

"Your note-taking, I mean."

A secretive look came over the child's flabby face, and her hand went unconsciously to the sporran. Glancing slantwise at Nigel, she said, "I'm going to give you an association test. I say a word, and you have to say the first word that comes into your head. You must—"

"Yes, I know how it's done."

Primrose drew the notebook from her sporran, opened a page, held her fountain pen poised, and began.

"Summer."

"Fields," responded Nigel.

"Love."

"Hate."

"Beetle."

"Dung."

"British."

"Hypocrisy."

"Salt."

"Lord Dunsany."

"What?" Primrose paused in the task of writing down Nigel's answers. "Lord who?"

"Dunsany. He was very fastidious about what kind of salt he ate. As far as I remember, rock salt was the only—"

"Oh, all right. Next word—Loin."

"Pork."

"Drown."

"Griefs."

"Ice cream."

"Hot chocolate sauce."

"Makarios."

There was a noticeably longer pause before Nigel replied, "Beard."

Primrose asked him a few more; but only as a formality, or to lull the unmasked EOKA agent, Nigel Strangeways, into a false sense of security. That pause after "Makarios" had given him away properly, judging by the veiled look of triumph on young Primrose's face. And Nigel had not made it deliberately; he could kick himself now, for as a result of that involuntary pause the child would be trailing him everywhere—yes, and anyone he talked to, since Bentinck-Jones had told her there were two EOKA agents on board. Damn the man for his fatuous games!

Ten minutes later, Nigel sat down in the saloon for breakfast. It was only five past seven, and the other occupants of the table had not yet arrived. Nigel ordered orange juice and coffee, and started in on the plate of buns before him, buttering them heavily. He noticed at other tables Jeremy Street, his head buried in a book, and Primrose Chalmers with a man and a woman—her parents, no doubt—who had the mildly lunatic look not uncommon among psychoanalysts, lay or otherwise.

When Clare turned up, she laid before him a copy of the *Journal of Classical Studies* and gave him a warm kiss. Nigel leafed through the magazine till he found what he was looking for. It was a long review of Jeremy Street's last translation—the *Medea:* it took that work to pieces with a chilly, relentless hostility, a derisive contempt, and a wealth of scholarship, which made Nigel positively blush for the unfortunate translator. The review was signed with the initials "I.A." No wonder Jeremy Street had bristled at the very mention of the name "Ambrose," and removed the *Journal* from the reading room. And, if Ianthe Ambrose treated her pupils' efforts in this devastating manner, it was small wonder that Faith Trubody should have blanched to see her coming on board.

There was a sharp rap on the table, and Nigel looked up. Clare had taken a piece of bread from the basket in front of her and nearly broken her teeth on it.

"What *is* this?" she asked, bashing it on the table again. "Pumice·stone?"

"It's Greek bread. The Greeks are a tough people. Try a bun instead."

"You've eaten them all."

"So I have. Never mind. Just listen to this." In a low voice Nigel read out the last two paragraphs of I.A.'s review:

From any translator we have the right to demand two minimum qualifications—an intimate knowledge of the language of the original, and a refined feeling for his own. If Mr. Street merely showed himself ignorant of modern textual recensions of his author, it would be deplorable enough. But when carelessness is added to ignorance, when a translation is defaced by solecisms, wild guesswork, and even by schoolboy howlers, when unjustifiable liberties are taken with the text, then no protest can be sufficiently strong. As for Mr. Street's command of his own language, we can only say that it is negligible. A version which, mixing stale colloquialisms with the most tawdry trappings of romanticism, substitutes vulgarity for grandeur, hysteria for tragedy, and has the effect of turning Medea into a suburban delinquent, may titillate the unlettered public but must degrade its original. In his preface, Mr. Street makes great play with his dislike for the "pedantry" of scholars. It is possible, however, that Euripides would prefer the strait jacket of scholarship to the poisonous shirt in which Mr. Street has clothed him.

We have had occasion before now to censure Mr. Street in these columns. To popularize the classics is one thing, to pervert them is another. The standards of translation are low enough today, in all conscience. A person of Mr. Street's influence, putting out work so shoddy and so slovenly as his *Medea,* is lowering the standards to a nadir hitherto unconceived. We can but repeat what Blake said of Sir Joshua Reynolds—"this man is hired to depress art."

"Gracious!" said Clare after an awed silence. "She doesn't seem to like him, does she?"

"She's given chapter and verse for all her criticisms, earlier on."

"Well, if somebody said that about my work, I'd kill her."

II

By eight o'clock that morning the *Menelaos* had anchored off Delos, and caiques were waiting to take the passengers ashore. There was an excited feeling of anticipation in the air: the passengers had loosened up, no longer exchanging formal introductions before they talked to strangers. Only the French contingent, forming as ever a sort of splinter group, waited on the promenade deck in a cluster and maintained an insular detachment. Nigel and Clare, near the head of the gangway, would be among the first to get off.

"Good morning, good morning," cried Mr. Bentinck-Jones, pushing his way up to them. "We're lucky in our weather. It's often too rough to disembark here, you know."

A sailor handed a landing card to each passenger, and soon they were chugging their way in a crowded motor caique to the quay.

"What's this? A reception committee?"

All along the quay figures could be seen, who presently resolved themselves into men, women, and children displaying their wares—bright-colored scarves, nuts, trinkets, rough-woven shirts, and shopping bags. The sun was beating down fiercely on the treeless island; the water beside the quay looked cool and deep green. Nigel noticed the Bishop of Solway purchasing and putting on a shirt of turquoise and white horizontal stripes, which gave him a remarkably piratical appearance.

Having run the gantlet of the island traders, the passengers straggled away from the sea toward the sites of the two cities, Greek and Roman, which covered the ground, almost as far as eye could see, with a litter of masonry. Lizards baked on the stones, skittering away into crannies when a footstep came too near. The parched brown grass rasped against one's shoes, and it was hard to believe that in springtime the island is thick with flowers.

Nikki now jumped up on a marble slab, and made a traffic policeman's gesture. Most of the party gathering around, and the stragglers at last arriving, Nikki announced through his hand megaphone that two brief talks would now be given. The celebrated British savant, Mr. Jeremy Street, would talk about the mythological significance of Delos, and Professor George Greenbaum, of Yale University, would then speak on the archaeological aspects. After this, the party would split up into small groups, which would be conducted over the site by the Greek guides.

The travelers disposed themselves as best they could, wherever a declivity or a broken pillar promised some shade. Jeremy Street, hatless, in royal-blue linen trousers and a pale-blue shirt, stood on the slab waiting for them to settle. He had waved aside the megaphone which Nikki preferred.

Whatever might be his defects as a scholar and a translator, it at once became evident that Jeremy Street was an exceptionally good lecturer. His voice carried clearly to the outer fringes of the crowd. He spoke without notes, without confusing digressions, without a trace of self-consciousness. One could admire his technique, thought Nigel, as one admired the phrasing of a first-rate professional singer, because it was masterly yet did not call attention to itself.

"We are on the Sacred Island," he began, "the legendary birthplace of Apollo and Artemis. Legend is an attempt of prescientific man to explain the world to himself, to solicit or appease the mysterious powers of nature. What did that many-sided deity, Apollo, represent to those who first, out of their fears, their needs and their aspirations, created him?" . . .

As the charming, resonant voice went on, Nigel glanced around the scattered audience. They were clearly spellbound. Only Ianthe Ambrose, sitting huddled up with her back against a mound, struck a discordant note. She was tweaking at a piece of wiry grass beside her, a sour and skeptical look on her face; perhaps it was the result of having just read her blistering article on Street's *Medea*, but Nigel got the impression of something more positive than skepticism—it was jealousy that lay barely concealed behind her sullen yet attentive expression, or was a remorseless hostility waiting in ambush there? He suddenly dreaded that she was going to make a scene, make some virulent attack upon the lecturer.

But, on this occasion, Ianthe Ambrose held her fire. Jeremy Street ended, was loudly applauded, and gave way to the American professor. During the latter's discourse, Nigel noticed Jeremy Street quietly perch himself on a piece of pavement close to the blond Faith Trubody, who looked up at him with an expression of shy but near-idolatrous admiration. It was noticeable, too, that when the audience split up into smaller groups, Street accompanied Faith and her father toward the Hall of the Bulls. Mr. Bentinck-Jones, who had started in another group, soon moved away from it and tagged onto them, talking assiduously.

"Poor little man, he doesn't like to feel left out of anything," Clare remarked. "Well, I'm going to concentrate on the lions."

Nigel knew from her tone that she wanted to be by herself for a while. So they arranged to meet at midday outside the café adjoining the museum, and struck off on separate paths. Nigel trailed along with the party that included Street and the Trubodys, visiting the Roman quarter, admiring the mosaic floor depicting Dionysus on a tiger, and then making his way up the stony track which led to Apollo's cave on Mount Kynthos. Halfway up, he saw Melissa Blaydon sitting alone on a rock. She signaled to him, and he went over to her.

"I've done an idiotic thing," she said; "broken my shoelace. You haven't got a piece of string?"

"I'm afraid not."

"Well, I must just sit here till help comes," she remarked cheerfully. It was odd, he thought, the way this mondaine creature looked as perfectly at home here as a lizard: her brown skin absorbed the fierce sunshine; she radiated vitality, but also a kind of coolness far more provocative than the stock female devices for attracting attention. She is Artemis, he thought, but what she hunts is men. Looking around, he realized that he was quite alone with her on the hillside.

"Perhaps if we picked some of these long wiry grass stems and plaited them, we could make a temporary shoelace?"

"Oh, what a resourceful man!" Melissa's eyes—greenish-brown, with gold flecks in one of them—dwelt lingeringly upon his. "Well, to work."

As he pulled the grass and she plaited it, she explained that her sister had not felt up to climbing the hill.

"I do hope this cruise will do her good."

"Yes. I'm rather worried about her. She seemed well over the worst before we started, and the doctor said it'd be quite all right for her to come. But—" Melissa's deep voice trailed away.

"But she's having a bit of a relapse?"

"I'm afraid so. Last night, after we left you, she got into a dreadful state—well, you know, saying she couldn't stand it any more—her loneliness—nothing worth living for."

"But she has you. You're extraordinarily patient and unselfish with her."

"Me? Unselfish?" Melissa laughed harshly. "My dear man, I'm about as selfish as any woman living. I'd not seen Ianthe for years. She and I never really hit it off, from the cradle. When I got the cable saying she was seriously ill, I flew from the Bahamas. But that, and bringing her on this cruise—well, I suppose it was just because I felt guilty for having neglected her so long. And for living among the fleshpots while she had to grind away at school."

"She's got a brilliant intelligence, I'd say."

"Oh yes, I suppose so."

"Why did the school sack her? Surely not for having a nervous breakdown."

"I don't know," said Melissa vaguely. "There was some row, I believe. They're a lot of catty old virgins, these schoolmistresses. Ianthe has taught at several schools. I expect they're jealous because she's so much cleverer than they are. And I dare say"—Melissa gave him her lopsided smile—"she let them know it."

"Well, I still think you're very good to her."

"Of course Ianthe's always been mad keen to visit Greece. All these ruins and things are wasted on me. I only hope she won't be distracted from them."

"Distracted?"

Melissa turned her head away. "She feels she must play gooseberry to me. I'm a year older than Ianthe actually; but she sort of invilig—what's the word?"

"Invigilates?"

"Yes, invigilates me, poor sweet." Melissa gazed at Nigel, her red lips parted. "I seem to be unbosoming to you an awful lot. Does everyone?"

"Absolutely everyone."

Melissa laughed. "Yet you don't seem a bit nosy—not like that Bentinck-Jones creature. Oh dear, here comes another horde of cultural pilgrims."

They talked a bit longer about Ianthe. Then Melissa, who had finished plaiting the grasses, threaded them through the eyeholes of her shoe. She arched a brown, pretty foot at Nigel, for him to put the shoe on.

"You'd better go easy with this. I don't know how long it will hold," said Nigel, gingerly knotting the grass plait.

"Walk down the hill with me, then. And if it breaks, you can support my feeble frame the rest of the way."

Melissa Blaydon evidently took it for granted that any man would alter his plans to suit her; she could hardly have forgotten that Nigel had been walking up the hill when they met. Yes, she's a "spoiled" woman, but this calm assumption that everyone will love to dance attendance on her is somehow quite inoffensive, thought Nigel.

This thought prompted him to say, as they descended the stony track, "I imagine you had a very good relationship with your father."

"Yes, I did. But how—?"

"And your sister didn't?"

Melissa made no reply. A strange look, both rueful and fretful, came over her face, shutting her away from him. Stumbling over a stone, she clutched his arm; the contact sent a sort of instantaneous flash right through his body.

"You're not offended?" he asked.

Still not looking at him, Melissa exclaimed, "Why can't one just be allowed to be happy, if that's one's nature?"

III

Clare, meanwhile, was concentrating on the lions. She had picked her way among the tumbled masonry, past a headless female figure in voluminous draperies, with her right arm, apparently, in a sling, beyond which a tall, four-pillared portico—all that was left of a temple—commanded the skyline. Columns, single or in groups, sprouted all over the site, a petrified forest blinding white in the glare of the sun. Near the Sacred Lake sat the five lions on their plinths. Their flat heads and gaping jaws, eroded by centuries of storm, gave them the appearance of sea lions; but the powerful forepaws on which they were propped, and the crouching strength of the haunches, had an almost naturalistic truth.

Had the man who carved them ever seen a lion? Clare wondered.

They sat there in a row, guardians, confident but alert, waiting—or so it struck Clare—for something to happen. They had waited a long time, in their calm, archaic poses. She singled out one of the lions, and directed all her attention upon it. The slightly curving diagonal line of the back, from head to tail—could one aim at that sort of simplicity nowadays without falling into a self-conscious primitivism?

As Clare intensely scrutinized the lion, its simple strength seemed to pass into her. She felt refreshed, reinvigorated, and wonderfully sleepy. Moving into the shadow of a wall nearby, she lay down and fell asleep.

She was awakened by voices that, through the daze of sleep, sounded unnaturally loud.

". . . don't intend to discuss the matter with you."

"I'm sorry, but you've got to."

"Are you threatening me? How dare you talk to me like this?"

"You know that my sister was very ill after— She had

brain fever. If she had died, it would have been your responsibility."

"That of course is ridiculous. I'm sorry to hear about her illness, but—"

"You made a vile accusation against her, and she was expelled. I happen to be very fond of Faith. She told me the whole story."

"Your loyalty does you credit. But it doesn't seem to occur to you that Faith might have made up whatever story she told you; we never found her very reliable, I'm afraid, where the truth was concerned." Ianthe Ambrose's voice was firm and cool, but there was a jagged edge to it.

"It wasn't just what you accused her of. You'd been picking on her all that term, though God knows why—she was supposed to be your favorite pupil before that. It's a wonder you didn't drive her to suicide."

"Oh, fiddlesticks! She was a clever girl, certainly. Scholarship standard. But we'd always found her rather unbalanced and rather deceitful. She was caught cheating—using test papers she had stolen from my room. On top of that, she was grossly insolent to me before the whole class. Those are the facts."

"I beg your pardon. That is your version of the facts. Faith's version is that you—you framed her."

Peter Trubody's young voice rose higher, and what he went on to say sounded all the more horrible for being uttered in the same clipped, refined, gobbling public-school accent.

"—framed her because you'd—" he plunged at it desperately—"you'd made advances to her and she wasn't having any of that."

There was a moment of absolute silence. Then Clare heard a violent crack. Miss Ambrose had slapped Peter's face.

"You'll regret this," the boy said presently, his voice quite low again, but still with the absurdly pompous senior prefect's intonation. "You see, I'm determined to clear Faith's name."

"Don't talk like a novelette."

"I know you're very clever and all that. But the truth always wins, in the end. No, you're not going yet. I shall take steps to see things put right, and you will not find the process very pleasant. It would be simplest all around if you wrote a confession—"

"This is utterly grotesque!"

"If you don't, you'll find that other people can be just as —as vindictive as you. I'm warning you."

"Let me go at once!"

"Not till— Does your sister know why you were sacked from the school last term? Oh yes, a friend of Faith's wrote to her about it. She said—"

"If you don't let go of me this instant, I'll call for help." Ianthe's voice wobbled on the edge of hysteria.

"I bet you will," said Peter contemptuously. "And accuse me of trying to rape you or something. Another false accusation. You're pretty handy with them, aren't you, Miss Ambrose? Very well, you can go now." The boy spoke like a prefect who has just ticked off a fag. "But I'd advise you to remember what I've said. You're going to pay for what you did to Faith. One way or another."

There was a noise of feet scrabbling on stones. A few sobbing breaths came from Ianthe. Peering around the end of the wall, Clare saw her and Peter Trubody move away in different directions, Ianthe stumbling among the stones. Clare also noticed the figure of Primrose Chalmers emerge from behind the nearest lion: the child was putting her notebook and pen into the sporran; the expression on her face was both complacent and puzzled, as if an entomologist had netted some exquisite but unidentifiable moth.

When she got up from the shadow of the wall, the meridian sun struck down at Clare's head like a hammer. But it was not the sun which made her feel sick.

Nigel was awaiting her outside the café. After disposing of an ice-cold orangeade, she felt better. The tables around them were all occupied.

"Let's go into the Museum," said Clare. "There's something I must tell you."

In a cool, empty gallery, among the stone-deaf ears of statues, she still kept her voice low as she told him what she had overheard just now.

"I don't know why it should have upset me so; it was all so unreal and melodramatic. But I felt quite sick. And that monster, Primrose, taking it all down."

"Well, it's one mystery cleared up. We know why Faith took on so when she saw Miss Ambrose coming aboard." Nigel glanced speculatively at Clare. "Which story do you believe?"

"Which story?"

"Ianthe's? Or the Faith-and-Peter version?"

"I don't know," said Clare slowly. "I dare say Ianthe could be vindictive—well, there's that review of Jeremy Street. And I dare say Faith Trubody is rather unbalanced. Nigel, he couldn't really do anything to her?"

"Peter? I shouldn't think so. Might start some sort of persecution campaign, perhaps. Awfully bad form for a public-school type like him." Nigel gave her a longer look this time. "What's on your mind, love?"

"Yes. You're quite right. It's what Ianthe might do to Peter that really worries me—if he did start 'taking steps,' as he called it, I mean. The woman isn't quite sane."

"Well, she's got Melissa looking after her. And there's a ship's doctor."

"Melissa won't be much help once she gets into her stride with the men." Clare peered clairvoyantly into Nigel's face. "Ah. She has already?"

"There are circumstances in which the male, however innocent, cannot refrain from looking guilty," Nigel proclaimed. "Yes, I was engaged with Melissa on the hillside while you were dropping eaves. I wouldn't say she is in full stride yet, but she's working up to it. She improves on closer acquaintance."

"Oh."

"She thinks I am very resourceful."

"She does, does she?"

"Yes. And she's afraid that her sister may commit suicide."

IV

After dinner that night there was to be a seminar in the forward lounge. The two lecturers who had spoken in the morning would be available to answer questions on the subject of Delos, and passengers were encouraged to contribute to the discussion.

To Nigel, who even as an undergraduate had never been conspicuous for attendance at lectures, this sounded far too much like work. So he and Clare settled down in deck chairs aft, thereby missing another scene of the drama which was gradually unfolding on the *Menelaos*.

They sat in companionable silence, thinking their own thoughts while the ship rolled in a moderate sea raised by the strong wind which so often, Mr. Bentinck-Jones had informed them, got up in these parts at nightfall. Clare was still brooding over her lion. Nigel fell to speculating about Melissa Blaydon. Pliant, charmingly acquiescent on the surface, she had, he suspected, a very tough core. Like Ianthe, she could be a ruthless remover of obstacles. Perhaps a more skillful and practiced one, too. But she had her contradictions; just after dinner Nigel had heard her say to Ianthe, "But, darling, it really isn't my thing at all. Why can't you go by yourself?" Ianthe had made some reply, inaudible to him; and then, a few minutes later, he had seen the sisters going into the seminar together. Melissa did seem capable of disinterested affection, of some unselfishness.

He was reminded now of something else she had told him on the hillside. Ianthe had always been an independent character, going her own way; and the sisters had corresponded little, over the years when Melissa was abroad. But, since Ianthe's breakdown, she had become dependent upon her sister. It was not merely that she hated letting Melissa out of her sight for long; she also never tired of asking Melissa about her life abroad, her marriage, her travels.

"Well," Nigel had said, "I suppose she gets a vicarious satisfaction out of it—the stay-at-home sister reveling in the romantic life of—"

"Of the Prodigal Daughter?" Melissa had cut in, with her lopsided smile. "I wonder. You see, Ianthe always despised the sort of life I've lived. She thinks I'm a feather-wit. I can't imagine why she should suddenly be so interested in it."

"Wouldn't that be an effect of her illness, and of losing her job? She feels there's a void that needs filling up; and even more, the need of a close relationship with someone. Isn't she just trying to re-create the bond between herself and you?"

At which, Melissa Blaydon had looked skeptical. . . .

Three-quarters of an hour later, the seminar being over, Clare and Nigel strolled into the A lounge forward, to be met by that particular kind of high-pitched buzzing which is given off by a beehive or a human community when it has been disturbed. Nigel got drinks at the crowded bar, then carried them over to a corner where Mrs. Hale was beckoning.

"My *dear,*" exclaimed the good lady, "what you have missed!"

"The seminar was interesting?" said Clare.

"Interesting! It was a riot." Mrs. Hale's eyes opened wide with shocked glee. "Miss Ambrose and Mr. Street pretty well had a stand-up fight."

"Oh, come now, my dear," the Bishop of Solway mumbled. "A bit of controversy, let's call it."

"Oh, I dare say it's nothing to the shindies that go on in Convocation. But to me it looked like an all-in intellectual wrestling match."

"But what happened?"

"Miss Ambrose got up and asked a question. Mr. Street answered it. She whipped in another; and before you could say 'Artemis,' they were at it hammer and tongs—something to do with Linear B. What on earth *is* Linear B? Sounds like trigonometry to me."

"It's a Greek script," said the Bishop. "Blegen found tablets at Pylos inscribed in Linear B, just before the war. Wace found others at Mycenae in 1952—the same year the script was deciphered as being in the Greek language. The discoveries proved Wace's theory that Mycenaean civilization was Greek, and that there was strong Mycenaean influence in the last phase at Knossos. Schliemann, of course—"

"My dear Edwin, do stick to the point," interrupted his wife. "The point is that Miss Ambrose was unforgivably rude to poor Mr. Street. She tried to humiliate him, in public, and—"

"I'm afraid she succeeded," said the Bishop to Nigel, in a grave tone. "She exposed some bad gaps in his knowledge —well, made him look like a badly taught schoolboy, in fact. It really was most unpleasant."

"And quite irrelevant?" asked Nigel.

"Irrelevant to a discussion on Delos, certainly. It looked to me regrettably like a piece of pure mischief on Miss Ambrose's part. I felt there was some personal animosity at work."

"Her sister was terribly embarrassed. Quite furious with Ianthe. In fact, she dragged her out of the seminar before she'd finished—"

"You mean, physically dragged her out?"

"Well, not quite. But Miss Ambrose was shaking all over, and—here comes the other duelist."

Jeremy Street, accompanied by Faith Trubody and her father, entered the lounge. There was a moment's silence; then everyone started talking, louder and faster, it seemed, than before. Faith, moving closer to Jeremy, looked around in a challenging way. The man's face flushed a little; the lips were tightly compressed. After getting their drinks, he and the Trubodys came across to a vacant group of chairs next to the Bishop's party.

"Well!" Mrs. Hale said without preamble. "I should think you need a drink after that. What a battle!"

Nigel gave her full marks for the genuine and unexpected tact she was showing by this open reference to the scene.

Jeremy Street gave a tight smile, which did not relax his face. "She's rather a pest, I'm afraid."

"It was absolutely typical of the Bross," put in Faith Trubody. "There's nothing she likes so much as showing up —" She broke off, flushing scarlet, and looking miserable at the gaffe. "Of course, I don't mean you—I mean, she's naturally a bloody-minded old schoolmarm and—" The girl floundered again. Jeremy Street made no attempt to help her out, Nigel noticed. Bad mark to him.

"My daughter was taught for a while by Miss Ambrose," said Mr. Trubody, a pleasant-faced man with gray hair and a manner of easy authority.

"And I was taught by Miss Ambrose's father—oh, some thirty years ago," said Jeremy Street. "He was my tutor at Cambridge. A very able man. She gets her talent from him. And"—Street made one of those delicate yet commanding gestures which had graced his lecture at Delos—"and her rather cantankerous disposition."

Jeremy Street's smile was calm, almost Olympian. He spoke without any trace of resentment. Is he quite invulnerable in his self-esteem, wondered Nigel, or is he putting on an act? Jeremy was, at any rate, one of those men whose public *persona* encases them so completely that the private self is invisible. What would one find underneath if the carapace were removed?

Nigel studied Faith Trubody, who in her turn was gazing raptly at Street as he talked, her mouth half open. The small, irregular teeth gave her a sly, vixenish look in profile. She was prettier than Nigel had thought, though; still quite unsure of herself, temperamentally erratic, he judged, and working up a full-blown crush on the handsome Jeremy

Street. Or was it a crush? Did she perhaps hope to enlist him in her brother's campaign against Ianthe Ambrose? And then, of course, there was the problem of Faith's expulsion from school. Peter Trubody, in Clare's hearing, had given one account of this, Miss Ambrose another; Nigel was by no means disposed to accept the former without question. Faith too, he thought, was quite capable of making false charges.

On an impulse, he asked the girl if she knew why Miss Ambrose had had to leave Summerton. Faith seemed rather taken aback, but replied:

"Well, I don't know—I mean, she had a nervous breakdown last term, but a friend of mine who's still there told me it was because the Bross was a failure as a teacher."

"But she's a first-rate scholar, I thought."

"Oh yes, but she can't sort of put it over. We weren't getting the university scholarships we should have been." Faith's green eyes flickered at Nigel. "And she wasn't popular, you know. She, well, had favorites, and ignored everyone else. And of course she was terribly sarcastic."

"Were you a favorite of hers?" Nigel asked, smiling.

"She got me sacked from the place."

It was no answer, but Nigel did not press the question. Their conversation had been conducted in low tones, while Jeremy Street and the Bishop talked about Cambridge. The pair made an interesting contrast: the Bishop, with his neat, vandyke beard, his rumpled gray alpaca suit, his Viking-blue eyes; Jeremy Street, dressed dandyishly, talking with the conscious stylishness of a belletrist, smoothing the golden hair which curled up at the nape of his neck. A rumbling bass voice, a resonant tenor.

Faith Trubody was gazing at Street now with open adulation. What most disquieted Nigel was that the man appeared to be unembarrassed by it—to accept it as his natural and rightful due. It might have been better for him, if not for Faith, that he should be a straightforward womanizer. But Jeremy Street was cold, Nigel feared—as cold as Narcissus.

Soon after ten o'clock, Clare feeling sleepy, she and Nigel took a turn around the deck before going to their cabins. The promenade deck was lined with deck chairs, nearly all of them occupied. As they passed, a woman's voice called:

"Oh, Miss Massinger, have you seen my sister anywhere?"

"No, Mrs. Blaydon. She's not in the big lounge, anyway." Clare moved closer to the figure huddled in the deck chair. "Oh, I'm sorry, Miss Ambrose. I mistook you for your sister. Shall I tell her you want her, if I see her?"

"Thank you."

In the stern of the *Menelaos*, very close together at the rail, Nigel presently noticed two figures. The broad back and black oiled hair of Nikki were unmistakable. The woman so close at his side was Melissa Blaydon.

"What do we do about it?" Clare whispered.

"Better tell her."

"Mrs. Blaydon. Your sister was asking for you. She's back there on the promenade deck."

Melissa swung around. Her eyes gradually focused, as if she were coming out of an anesthetic. Her nostrils were distended.

"What? Oh, thank you. I'd better go, Nikki."

She gave the man a quick, deep glance, then hurried away.

Nikki gazed after her with frank admiration. "What a woman!" he then exclaimed, shining his teeth at Nigel and Clare. "It is sad that she has—what does your poet call it? —an albatross around her neck."

V

The next morning, they landed on Patmos. Led by Nikki, the main party straggled from the quay, past groups of children holding up flowers, to a tree-lined square on the island side of the little port. Here the donkeys were congregated which would convey them up to the monastery of St. John the Divine.

Here, Ivor Bentinck-Jones was in his element. He helped the women onto their mounts, fussed over the harness, and encouraged the departing riders with cries of "Up and at 'em!" "Canyons to left of them, canyons to right of them!" "She'll be coming up the mountain when she comes!" and other appropriate slogans of the day.

Nigel, who had seen Clare and Mrs. Hale jog off, found himself at the end of the cavalcade. He eyed his own animal with considerable misgiving. It seemed several sizes too small for him, and it had a distrait yet purposeful look in its rolling eye which reminded him of the wrong kind of society hostess. On mounting, he found his misgivings only too well justified. The stirrups were so short that he could only keep his feet in them by bending his legs backward, so that he was trussed like a chicken, while two pieces of metal, projecting from the ancient saddle, drove viciously into his thighs if he attempted to grip with them. For reins, the animal had a single rope, so that, in order to change direction, Nigel must lean forward and pass the rope over the brute's muzzle to the other side of its head.

As well as these handicaps, Nigel discovered, when the ass's owner gave his bloodcurdling cry and thumped the animal on its hind quarters, that it had a bias like a bowl; or else an inveterate feud with Bentinck-Jones's donkey. As they went side by side up the stony track, Nigel's ass kept boring into his companion's, as if determined to force it over the edge.

Bentinck-Jones, however, was unruffled. "Sure-footed animals. Just leave them to find their own way," he brightly remarked as his own beast, driven by Nigel's into the shallow ditch at the side of the track, stumbled over a heap of stones. And a minute later, his pudgy face pink and sweating, "I say, Strangeways, what about Miss Ambrose, eh?"

"Well, what about her?"

"Obstinate. Nikki and her sister both tried to persuade her not to come up to the monastery. Rough journey. Very exposed to the sun. But no, she would do it."

"She's paid to see the monastery, so—"

"Mrs. Blaydon's paid, you mean. She's footing the bill, you know. Quite inseparable, aren't they?"

"Who?" asked Nigel, holding onto the saddle for dear life as the asses suddenly decided to gallop.

"Ah-ha! Who indeed?" panted Mr. Bentinck-Jones, giving him a disagreeable wink. Clashing together in midtrack, the asses slowed again to a walk. Their owner howled at them, and they broke into a bone-jolting jog trot.

"Handsome fellow, Nikki. Virile, eh?" said Ivor Bentinck-Jones. "Quite the lady-killer. Rather a bad show, though, don't you think?"

"What's a bad show?" Nigel was deliberately obtuse.

"Well, he's in an official position. Cruise manager. Looks bad. Do you think he's made her yet?"

Appalled by this sudden vulgarity, Nigel said nothing. Ivor seemed undeterred, however. Beaming benignly, he cooed, "Ah well, these shipboard romances. Ships that pass in the night. But of course they're not the only unmarried couple on board."

Conscious of the man's sharp, sideways glance, Nigel pretended confusion. "What do you mean by that?" he asked jerkily.

"Well, there's young Miss Trubody and our distinguished lecturer, Jeremy Street."

Nigel feigned indignation, and relief. "Oh, come! He's old enough to be her—"

"It's a case," Ivor jovially proclaimed. "That girl's just ripe to fall off the bough, mark my words. But that sort of thing is dangerous for a man in a public position. Or," he added, "a woman."

"But Miss Trubody isn't a public figure."

"I wasn't thinking of la Trubody, old man," said Bentinck-Jones in his coziest way.

A pandemonium of cries and clattering hoofs broke out

from above, where the track zigzagged down the hillside from the fortress-like monastery and the ruff of white houses around its base, now only a quarter of a mile away. The donkey men, having deposited their first customers, were racing the animals down the hill to pick up more. The track was narrow, and it was impossible to get off it on either side at this point.

The avalanche of asses poured down, bringing with them a cloud of dust and a torrent of stones, cannoning onto Nigel and his companion as they pressed to the side of the track. Stimulated by the general excitement, Nigel's ass suddenly swerved against its old enemy, and Bentinck-Jones was thrown off and went rolling down the slope. This, fortunately, was not steep here. A rock arrested his descent and, clambering up onto the track, he remounted. He wore on his face the pertinaciously cheerful expression of the butt of the party determined to show that he takes horse-play in good part.

As they moved on again, Nigel said to him mildly, "Pride, it seems, is not the only thing that goes before a fall."

"What's that? Don't get you, old man." Ivor's eyes had lost their habitual twinkle.

"Never mind. Sorry about the bumping and boring. I simply can't steer this animal with one rope."

"Oh, that's all right, Strangeways. I shan't need to sue for compensation, I hope." There was the faintest stress on the word "sue." "I always prefer friendly arrangements, don't you?"

"Fall heavily, but let off lightly? That sort of thing?"

"Could be. It all depends."

"It's nice to find you unbowed, though bloody. Depends on what?"

"On how much there is, shall we say, to lose." Bentinck-Jones pointed to a group standing at the foot of the steps leading up through the village. "Ah, there's Miss Massinger. Charming woman. Great talent. Genius. I hear there's talk of her being commissioned to do a portrait bust of royalty. Damn good show!"

"And there's the Chalmers child," said Nigel, his pale blue eyes fastened non-committally on Ivor Bentinck-Jones's small gray ones. "She reminds me of Wordsworth."

"Wordsworth? Good Lord!"

"You remember the lines?—'A Primrose by the river's brim A simple sucker was to him.'"

For once, Mr. Bentinck-Jones appeared to find himself at a loss for words; and when they had dismounted, he moved away, looking thoughtful. Primrose Chalmers glanced at his retreating back, her face dead-pan under the Venetian gondolier's hat.

In the courtyard of the monastery, the Bishop spoke for twenty minutes on the Orthodox Church. The Greek guides then took parties to view the dark and opulent chapel, the library with its 735 Byzantine MSS., and other features of the establishment. Nigel noticed that he and Clare were being shadowed everywhere by Primrose. No doubt the child was expecting him to hold some sinister communication with one of the monks; there were many of them—handsome, bronzed men, who smiled engagingly at their visitors, and with their beards, tall hats, and cassocks might have been doubles of Bishop Makarios. Primrose, judged Nigel, was a good deal more harmless following him around than spying on some of his fellow-travelers. Still, the child was a nuisance; and when they had emerged onto the monastery roof, to look at the incredible panorama of sea and islands spread out below them, Nigel moved over to her.

"How's the Elephant's Child today?" he asked.

"Do you mean me?"

"Yes. The Elephant's Child was possessed of insatiable curiosity."

"Oh?"

The Just-So Stories were evidently not required reading in the Chalmers household; undesirable to encourage animal fetishism.

"You know, I really am *not* an EOKA agent in disguise," Nigel said, seriously and kindly.

Primrose stared at him with a stony expression. Then a sly look came over her face.

"Oh, that!" she said contemptuously. "Do you think I really believe such rot?"

"You did at first, didn't you?"

"All that spy stuff is just compensatory fantasy building. I soon saw through it."

"Let's hope it's nothing worse."

Primrose looked sly and secretive again. Nigel took a shot in the dark.

"And now you've got better fish to fry?"

"I don't know what you mean."

"Curiosity," said Nigel, "can be an admirable thing. It can also be dangerous. It killed the cat."

"What cat?"

Nigel gave it up. The fat child just stood there, gazing at him through her thick spectacles, answering him in her flat, pedantic voice, like a Dictaphone playing back a conversation. It seemed impossible to make any human contact with her.

Later, Nigel was sorry that he had not persevered.

VI

A little before midday, the party went down the mountain to look at the cave where St. John, in exile, is believed to have written the Book of Revelation. The cave was very dark; and not till their eyes were accustomed to the darkness did they perceive that it had been made into a church. The low ceiling, the uneven floor, the gleam of an ikon, the voices subdued to whispers—one felt at the center of a mystery here.

The Bishop of Solway gave a short address, read a passage from the Book of Revelation, his deep voice rumbling through the gloom like a river rolling boulders, then asked them to join with him in a prayer. He had barely begun the prayer when a woman's voice broke out into a wild, muttering gabble, which sounded unnaturally loud in the hollow place.

"Take me out, Mel! I can't stand it! The dark, it's so dark. Make him stop! Let me out—it's like being buried alive!"

There was a shocked hush; then a scuffling sound as Mrs. Blaydon took her sister out of the cave. The Bishop, who had paused, began his prayer again; the strong voice, the noble words came like a purification, the *amen* they all uttered was very far from perfunctory.

When they came out of the cave-church, Nigel asked the Bishop to walk down to the port with him.

"I'm worried about Miss Ambrose," he said, as they started off.

"Should you not leave her case to Dr. Plunket?" the Bishop replied a little formidably; then smiled. "Or to the Church?"

"I think she's in need of both. But there are other aspects." Nigel hesitated. Then, drawing a certain document from his wallet, he handed it to the Bishop. "This is confidential, of course."

"What's this? . . . Oh, from the Assistant Commissioner C. . . . Well, I'd never have thought you moved in that world. But, my dear fellow, surely Miss Ambrose is not a criminal?"

"Not to my knowledge. But I'm afraid of worse unpleasantness breaking out on this cruise, unless— Look here, sir, I'd be very grateful if you would tell me what you know about Miss Ambrose and her sister, when they were children. You said, at dinner the other night, it was a sad story."

The Bishop of Solway gave Nigel a piercing scrutiny from beneath his bushy eyebrows. What he saw seemed to satisfy him.

"Very well, if you think it might help. E. K. Ambrose and I were Fellows of St. Teresa's for some years, before I took up parochial work. He was married—didn't live in College; but I saw quite a lot of his family. Melissa must have been —oh, about seven when I first met her; Ianthe was a year younger. The mother died giving birth to Ianthe."

"Ah."

"Yes. It explains a good deal. E.K. could never prevent himself feeling resentment against Ianthe—and, I'm afraid, showing it. Mind you, he tried to be fair, but there was a coldness in his attitude toward her; she was a sensitive child, and she must have noticed the efforts he made to be fair. I'm sure she felt shut out."

"Whereas Melissa was the reigning favorite?"

"Yes. She was an artful puss—could twist old E.K. around her little finger."

"And much more attractive to look at, I suppose."

"Oh, I don't know. They were both pretty children. Very much alike then, in fact. But Melissa had those coaxing ways. And Ianthe had killed the mother. So there it was."

"Ianthe tried to level the balance by appealing to the scholar in her father," suggested Nigel.

"You're very perceptive. Yes. It was rather pathetic, you know. She was always much cleverer than her sister. She learned to read quicker, and so on. She used to come and lay her little intellectual triumphs at E.K.'s feet. And he couldn't really accept them—he had to *pretend* interest and enthusiasm, and she'd see through it. She tried so many ways of getting at his heart."

"Stealing, no doubt?"

"Yes, I'm afraid that was one of them. The phase didn't last long. Clowning was another. She was an extraordinarily good mimic, and she used to imitate dons who came to the house, to make E.K. laugh. That did win him, but only while the performance lasted. Yes, she was a bright little thing; but strained, anxious, even in those days; trying too hard you know—permanent frown on her forehead. I say, I'm babbling on rather, aren't I?"

"Not a bit. Did she try becoming a boy?"

"What? Oh, I see what you mean. Yes, that came later, I seem to remember. She started playing games a lot. Riding. Tennis. Caddying for her father. That sort of thing. And of course she'd begun Latin and Greek very young.

But it didn't work. It's sad, when a child wants love as desperately as that, and—"

"How about Melissa? Did she and Ianthe hit it off?"

The Bishop hesitated. "It's so long ago. I don't remember them quarreling. But I doubt if they were ever close. They hadn't much in common, after all. And everything was so easy for Melissa—except, of course, the intellectual life; and she had no need of that."

"So she got thoroughly spoiled?"

"Well, it isn't good for anyone to have things coming too easily. I'm all for a few frustrations in childhood. And later. Doesn't do to feel yourself the center of the universe. Which is what she was, for E.K. Apart from his studies, I mean—they took first place."

The two fell silent for a minute, negotiating a rough section of the track. Then Nigel said meditatively, "And now Melissa is a rich widow, and Ianthe a failed schoolmistress. Nothing succeeds like success."

From under the beetling gray eyebrows, the Bishop gave him another keen look.

"I don't understand what you expect to do with all this past history."

"Ah, if it were *past* history—" Nigel broke off. "I don't even know, myself. I'm inquisitive about people, and I tend to get involved with them," he went on slowly. "I've spent a lot of my life dabbling in criminology. I've helped to hang quite a few murderers. But I've never yet prevented a crime."

"But what crime do you imagine you might prevent here?"

"If I knew *that*—I just feel there's too much explosive material lying about on the *Menelaos.*"

"Can I do anything?" asked the Bishop in his forthright way.

"You can pray," said Nigel seriously. "In particular, for Ianthe Ambrose."

VII

The bathing place was already crowded when Nigel and Clare, after a leisurely lunch under trees outside a little restaurant, arrived there. Some of the passengers were still exploring Patmos; a few had returned to the ship; but most of them, having collected their bathing clothes and picnic lunches from the quay, had made their way to the beach some time ago.

Nigel had a theory that, since the digestive processes do not start work till forty minutes after a meal, it was perfectly in order to bathe during this period. The water was deliciously warm, with so much salt in it that one was buoyed up and cushioned on the silky surface. He swam out fifty yards, then turning over lay on the sea, his eyes closed against the glare of the sun, his mind a blank. Nikki drove past him at a powerful crawl, his black head sleek as a seal's. The shouts and laughter of the bathers seemed to come, muted, through a haze of distance. Like a voice heard in a trance, a line from *Lucrece* irrationally repeated itself in Nigel's brain— *'Tis double death to drown in ken of shore.* Vaguely disturbed, he swam back to dry land.

Where he got out, Ianthe Ambrose was sitting, huddled up with her back against a rock.

"Not going in?" he asked pleasantly.

"I can't swim."

"It's quite shallow for a bit, you know."

"And I'm afraid of the sea urchins."

Nikki had warned the passengers, before their first bathe at Delos, to watch out for these unpleasant creatures, which leave their spines broken off in one's flesh, like splinters of glass, if one treads on them.

"Oh, I don't think there'd be any here," said Nigel. "You only get them on rocks, and you can see them through the water—black patches on white rocks."

Miss Ambrose shuddered, though she did not seem to have paid much attention. Her eyes, screwed up against the sunlight, were fixed on some point beyond him. Nigel followed her seaward gaze, and saw Melissa Blaydon, in her distinctive saffron-yellow bathing helmet, throwing a beach ball to Peter Trubody. He threw it back. The ball went wide, and Melissa swam a dozen swift effortless strokes to retrieve it.

"Your sister swims well."

"She has all the social graces," Ianthe tartly replied.

"Is that her Aqua-Lung?" asked Nigel, pointing to an object lying near at hand.

"No. I believe it belongs to that boy—what's his name?"

"Peter Trubody?"

"Yes."

Ianthe Ambrose seemed as difficult to make contact with as Primrose Chalmers, who sat a few paces away with her parents, reading a book, her stomach bulging in a tight blue swimming suit. Primrose, he thought, will grow up to be another Ianthe, if she isn't careful. There was something physically repugnant to him, alike in the precocious child and the unbalanced woman: their pasty faces, pebbly eyes, ungainly bodies. Why must Ianthe sit sweating in a woolen jumper and tweed skirt, martyring herself and making this everlasting tacit demand on her sister?

Ashamed of his physical reaction, Nigel tried again.

"The Bishop spoke well at the monastery, didn't he?"

"Oh, *he* knows his stuff," Ianthe ungraciously replied. Then her fingers began to writhe on her lap. "I'm told I made an exhibition of myself in that cave afterward."

"It's a pretty claustrophobic place," said Nigel gently.

"Huh! But nobody else started kicking and screaming there. No. It had to be me," she added dismally.

"Well, you've been ill, you can't expect to—"

"I know what you're really thinking," she burst out. "You're thinking that I exploit my illness. Just a hysterical, exacting female. Everybody thinks so. Melissa. Everybody."

"Oh, no, no." Nigel was dismayed. The woman was as prickly as a sea urchin. She disregarded his protest.

"But they'll feel differently when I'm gone"—the woman was muttering to herself now; oblivious of Nigel—"that'll teach them a lesson, all these womanizers and bores and rich harlots—"

"So you're thinking of suicide?" Nigel's voice was so frigidly dispassionate that it had the effect of a douche of cold water on Ianthe. She stopped ranting and stared at him in amazement.

"Well! I must say!"

Giving her no pause to recover, talking in the same emotionless tone, Nigel said, "How do you propose to do it?"

"Do be quiet! People can hear you."

"No one's listening. Are you going to kill yourself, or provoke someone else into doing it for you?"

"I—this is fantastic. You must be mad."

"There's young Peter. And Jeremy Street. Both itching for your blood. Have you made any other enemies recently? Or are you your own worst enemy?"

What effect this shock treatment might have had on Ianthe, he was unable to judge; for Melissa and Peter Trubody came walking out of the sea toward them. Peter was gazing at Melissa like a dog at its mistress. When he noticed Ianthe, he gave a curt nod, picked up his Aqua-Lung, and moved away.

"Hello, hello!" said Melissa gaily. "Well, I've done my bit by the Youth Club. Now I can relax."

She was wearing only a bikini. She could afford to. Her brown skin was flawless, unwrinkled still. The broad hips and the opulent slope of the haunches contrasted with her rather narrow shoulders, but such was her grace of movement, as she walked up the beach, that she gave the impression of perfect symmetry.

"Do put this on, Mel," said Ianthe, throwing her sister a beach robe. "That get-up may be all very well on the Riviera, but the Greeks don't like it."

"How do you know what the Greeks don't like?" Melissa

good-humoredly replied. Ianthe turned her head sharply away. She thinks Melissa is referring to Nikki, Nigel reflected; oh dear, oh dear.

Melissa had taken her lipstick and mirror out of a wicker basket, rectangular-shaped like an attaché case, and was touching up her full lips. Everything was so normal. Nigel could hardly believe that his recent conversation with Ianthe had taken place.

"Have you been using my scissors, darling?" asked Melissa, rummaging in the basket.

"What? To open my veins with? Of course not."

"Don't be silly. Oh, here they are." She turned to Nigel, holding up a bunch she had taken from the basket. "Have some grapes?" The robe falling open, her body seemed to be preening itself at him: her mouth quivered at the corners, her eyes held him so that it felt like a strenuous physical effort to drag his own away. For a few seconds this pose of shameless, almost aggressive, invitation was sustained; then Melissa withdrew, as it were, behind her own frontiers.

She just can't help it, said Nigel to himself as he walked away presently, eating the last few grapes; maybe she's hardly conscious of what she's doing. Lilith, the temptress. A dangerous, primeval force.

Clare was sitting in a group of people—Faith Trubody and her father, Jeremy Street, and the ubiquitous Bentinck-Jones—higher up the beach. Faith was not so prepossessing in bathing costume, which revealed the thinness of her arms and legs, the bony knobs of the collarbones, and the rounded shoulders. But her freckled face, as she chattered to Jeremy, had the charm of ingenuousness and animation.

"Have you seen Peter?" asked Mr. Trubody, as Nigel joined the party.

"He's gone off somewhere with his Aqua-Lung."

"He said he wanted to try it off those rocks; there's deep water," Faith told them.

"I do hope he'll watch out for the sea urchins. He's such a reckless boy."

"Oh, don't be absurd, Daddy!" Faith turned again toward Street, whose bronzed, oiled body was stretched full length beside her. "Are you *never* going in, Jeremy?"

"I prefer Apollo to Poseidon," said the distinguished lecturer lightly.

"The water's absolutely dreamy. And I bet you're a super swimmer."

Jeremy Street's smile was almost a smirk. He seemed able to lap up any amount of this schoolgirlish flattery. Nigel suspected that Street's preference for Apollo might be due to his deficiency as a swimmer, and his vanity would not allow him to betray even this in public.

"Well, I'm going in again," announced Bentinck-Jones. "You coming, Miss Trubody?"

"No. Not yet."

Ivor was an absurd spectacle, scampering down to the water on his short legs. But, once in the sea, he showed himself extremely proficient.

"Silly little man," said Faith pettishly. "Why does he hang around all the time?"

"He's an emotional parasite." Jeremy Street's tone, like a thin, immature claret, set Nigel's teeth on edge. "No life of his own, presumably. So he has to attach himself to others. Hence all this spurious vitality."

"What does the fellow do for a living?" Mr. Trubody asked.

"I gathered from him, on the train to Venice—he attached himself to me for some reason—that he had some sort of export business. He's not tried to sell me anything yet, however—except, of course, himself."

"Or to sell you *back* anything?" murmured Nigel.

Jeremy's eyes were concealed by sunglasses. "Sell me *back?* I don't follow you. But the procedures of the business world are all Greek to me—except that I know Greek."

"Ah. Christopher Fry," Mr. Trubody put in. "We businessmen are not all Philistines, you know, Street."

"No indeed," returned Jeremy, with a negligent, graceful wave of the hand. "I find that the most enlightened patronage of the arts comes from big industrial concerns nowadays. But there is plenty of room for extension." Street's voice itself had a note of patronage which Nigel found insufferable.

They were still discussing the subject when Faith cried out, "What's the matter, Peter?"

The boy was walking toward them along the beach, his face dead white and grim.

"Just somebody tried to drown me," he said, throwing the Aqua-Lung at his father's feet.

"Drown you? What do you mean?" Faith exclaimed.

"I did a deep dive, and found the Aqua-Lung wasn't working. Look. See the hole in the tube here?"

"It must have got damaged—"

"Damaged my foot! I know for a fact it was all right when I used it an hour ago. Somebody's bored a hole in it. Damn near suffocated me before I got to the surface again."

"May I see it?" asked Nigel.

"Here you are. And I know who did it, what's more. When I went in with Mrs. Blaydon, I left it—"

"Just a minute, Peter," interrupted Nigel, with such authority in his voice that the boy stopped short. "I'd like a word with you."

He took Peter aside to an empty part of the beach.

"Before you go and start another row with Miss Ambrose, remember that she is in precarious health, mentally, and also that you've no proof—the Aqua-Lung was lying about for some time where anyone could get at it."

"I have no intention of starting a row with Miss Ambrose, certainly not in front of Mel—her sister," said Peter with the stiff pompousness of his age. "I merely want to ask her a simple question: did you or didn't you tamper with this equipment?"

"And if she says no?"

"Well, I—I—"

"Exactly. You can't do anything more about it, my dear chap."

"But it's absolutely outrageous," spluttered the boy, in the exact tone he would be using thirty years later in his club to inveigh against the enormities of the budget. "The woman must be off her head."

"Could you make this hole with the point of a pair of nail scissors?"

"I should think so. If you persevered. The rubber's quite thick. Why?"

"In that case, it's possible that Miss Ambrose did do it."

"Well then!"

Nigel gazed non-committally at the smoldering eyes in the white face. A lock of wet hair flopped over the boy's brow. "You don't seem to ask yourself the obvious question."

"The obvious question?"

"Yes. *Why* should she do it?"

Peter Trubody avoided his eye. "Because she's mad, of course."

"Not to get in her blow first, so to speak?"

"What on earth—?"

"Well, you threatened her. You told her you were 'going to take steps' and 'other people could be vindictive too.' "

"Look here," the youth blustered. "Who the devil are you? Do you spend your time listening in to private conversations?"

"Oh, come off it! I've no tolerance for righteous—or un-righteous—indignation. You made nasty threats to a sick woman—no, never mind what she's done, or you believe she's done, in the past. If you must carry on a blood feud, don't start moaning when your opponent takes a poke at you."

"I wasn't moaning, blast you. I absolutely fail to see—"

"There's a great deal you absolutely fail to see, old son:

for example, that Ianthe Ambrose is not the kind of woman who can be bulldozed into giving you what you want to get from her."

"I suppose I ought to appeal to her better nature?" the youth sneered. "She hasn't got one. Ask Faith. If you knew as much—"

"I know that you're playing with dynamite," said Nigel gravely.

"An absolutely foul—a great wrong was done to my sister. I'm going to see that it's righted."

Oh lord! thought Nigel, he's just like one of those windy politicians proclaiming, "We shall not sheathe the sword until . . ."

"You're sure you're not confusing justice with revenge?" he quietly asked.

For a moment Peter Trubody looked indecisive; then, his face set and stubborn again, he walked off without another word.

Annihilation

A NUMBER OF PASSENGERS were up on the sun deck below
the bridge when, at nine o'clock next morning, the *Menelaos* steamed in toward Kalymnos. This island, some guidebooks claim, is the most beautiful of the Dodecanese. The
harbor lies in a broad, deep bay, above which tiers of
houses climb the hillsides. Clare Massinger's eyes were fastened upon the part of the town which rose up over the
port bow. The distance, the sunlight, and the steepness of
the hill produced a forshortening effect—a lack of perspec-
tive which made the whole thing less like a town than the
picture of a town: a picture by Ghika. The houses lay on the
background in cubes of brilliant color, white, sky blue,
Rickett's blue, and the purity of these blues and whites
gave the scene a primitive innocence which Clare found
enchanting.

" 'Where every prospect pleaseth and only man is vile,' "

announced the fat voice of Ivor Bentinck-Jones at her side.

"Oh, good morning," said Clare. "Yes, it's very strange and suitable. But do you think man is vile, or viler here than anywhere else?"

"Just a manner of speaking, dear lady."

Clare had no tolerance for the "dear lady" stuff.

"I wish poets would think before they speak," she said, a little irritably. Then, seeing Ivor's crestfallen expression, she relented. "Do you suppose it's town planning? I can't imagine the Greeks allowing themselves to be town-planned."

"I don't quite—"

"Those houses. All painted white or blue."

"Oh, that was started during the Italian occupation. They painted the town in the Greek colors as a protest, and they've kept it so ever since."

"Good for them. If they'd been Communists, they'd have painted the town red, I suppose."

Ivor gave a sycophantic chuckle. "Are you going to grace the ball tonight?" he presently asked.

"I expect I shall come to the dance."

"Then perhaps I may have the honor of—"

"Ah, that depends on Mr. Strangeways," said Clare, in a gush of mad irresponsibility. "He's appallingly *jealous*, you know."

Mr. Bentinck-Jones's face took on an attentive, inward look.

"Oh yes," Clare babbled on, "a man made a pass at me once during a dance, and Nigel didn't like it, and the man had to be taken to the hospital—twelve stitches in his face and two broken ribs. Of course, it was hushed up; the man happened to be connected with royalty."

"With royalty? Indeed?" Ivor had been regarding Clare suspiciously during this rigmarole. He soon moved away — presumably to swallow and digest her story, if he could.

Clare noticed Melissa Blaydon and Nikki leaning over the rail together: Ianthe Ambrose was in a deck chair not far off. Nikki appeared to be pointing out some spot on the coastline away to the left of the harbor; his fingers moved as if tracing a route to it from the town. What caught Clare's idle attention was a certain restraint in Nikki's gestures, an air of secrecy in the way he glanced around from time to time as if to make sure he was not overheard. But, if the pair were planning an assignation, they would hardly do it with Ianthe in earshot.

Yet today might well be their first opportunity. There were no important cultural objectives on Kalymnos; so, until the lecture tonight, and the dance that was scheduled to follow it, Nikki would have few official duties.

The *Menelaos* dropped anchor. Her steam whistle bellowed and a lazy echo came back from the hills. Ianthe Ambrose jerked convulsively at the noise, then buried her ears in her hands. A few minutes later, craft put out from the harbor to take off the passengers.

Nigel and Mrs. Hale joined Clare on the sun deck, watching the primitive-looking craft approach. Nikki came up and greeted them.

"What do we do here?" asked Mrs. Hale.

"You must buy a sponge, madam," Nikki replied. "I will personally select one for you. There's no need to pay more than—"

"But I can't spend all day buying a sponge."

"The island of Kalymnos makes its chief industry spongefishing," continued the cruise manager. "No less than three thousand of its male inhabitants pursue the avocation. They are absent all the summer diving for sponges on the coast of North Africa. Then"—a dazzling smile lit up his face—"after a few years, they kick the bucket. Lung disease. You know? Very sad."

"Well, when I have bought my sponge?"

"There is transportation waiting to take you to the bathing beaches. Mighty fine bathing here. Or you can explore the island on foot. The inhabitants are friendly. You know? They like to see tourists." Nikki beamed again, and his

American accent became more pronounced. "Yeah, in a dead-alive hole like this they sure do like to have visitors come along."

"Good for trade, eh?" said Nigel.

"Yup. And human interest. Oh boy!" Nikki replied with a rollicking laugh. "Well, I'll be seeing you."

"I should think there's a good deal of human interest available among the female population, with three thousand males absent all the summer," Mrs. Hale dryly remarked.

Nikki, reflected Clare, seems to be in a state of even greater euphoria than usual; it really does look as if he'd made an assignation with Melissa. But how do they propose to get rid of Ianthe?

II

"Why do we have to have these absurd landing cards? I know I shall lose mine one day," exclaimed Mrs. Blaydon.

"Red tape. Pure red tape," Mr. Bentinck-Jones snorted.

The flat, pedantic voice of Primrose Chalmers was heard. "Landing cards are a convenience," she announced. "If we didn't have them, it would be necessary to show our passports every time we went ashore."

"Why does this wretched child keep following us about?" muttered Ianthe, all too audibly.

"I'm not following you. I'm standing in the queue behind you. Landing cards are also useful so that the purser can check up whether all the passengers who disembarked returned to the ship. I should have thought that was obvious."

"Don't be insolent, little girl!" Ianthe snapped.

"I was just stating the facts."

"I'm sure my daughter had no intention of offending you," said Primrose's mother in a soothing voice. Ianthe was far from being soothed.

"When I want to be lectured to by schoolgirls, I will ask for it," she said, her face twitching.

The Chalmers parents remained impassive. This sort of resistance was a commonplace to lay analysts; one felt that a steam roller could pass over them without crushing them. Primrose, however, was less impervious to neurotic outbursts; she gave Ianthe's back an extremely baleful look, and seemed about to renew the controversy.

At this point, however, the queue began to move toward the gangway. Melissa, holding her wicker case in one hand, helped her sister down the steep incline.

Nigel Strangeways, meanwhile, had been taken aside by Mr. Trubody, and brought to a quiet corner of the lounge. The father of Faith and Peter was a distinguished-looking elderly man with a white mustache and the brisk, authoritative manner of the business tycoon.

"You're not going ashore at once?" It was less a question than a statement, though courteously delivered.

"No. We've got all day here."

"I wanted to have a word with you about Peter. I don't know what you said to him yesterday afternoon, but—"

"He hasn't told you?"

Mr. Trubody smiled. "I'm not always in Peter's confidence. But I can guess. It's a bit of a headache. He swears Miss Ambrose damaged his Aqua-Lung, and he wants me to have it out with her."

"I see."

"There are wheels within wheels here. You see, Peter and Faith are twins, and very close to each other. Peter has got it into his head that Miss Ambrose was behind Faith's having to leave her school last year—I mean, that Miss Ambrose did it out of some personal spite."

"And what do you think yourself?"

"I was far from satisfied by the headmistress's account of things. But I was not in a position to fight the case, so I had to take Faith away."

"And now Peter is doing the fighting, a guerrilla campaign?"

Mr. Trubody looked just a little huffy. He had had his children late in life, and now as a widower was inclined to spoil them or let them go their own way, Nigel surmised; the twins were by no means a wholly favorable testimonial to their upbringing.

"Guerrilla campaign? Surely that's putting it a bit too strongly, Strangeways?"

Nigel decided against telling Trubody yet what Clare had overheard at Delos. "Peter wants justice done to his sister, he told me. I'm not sure how scrupulous he would be in forwarding the good cause," said Nigel cautiously.

"There's nothing vicious about the boy. Are you suggesting—?"

"You saw the hole in the tube of the Aqua-Lung?"

"Certainly."

"Do you think it could have been bored by a small pair of nail scissors? In twenty minutes, say?"

"What's in your mind?" asked Mr. Trubody, glancing shrewdly at him.

"There's a possibility that Peter could have made the hole himself."

"But—but that's a fantastic suggestion. Sheer melodrama."

"The young can be melodramatic. And is it any less fantastic to suppose that Miss Ambrose did it, tried to drown your son?"

"The woman is unbalanced."

"I agree. But I doubt if she could have made that hole with nail scissors. Are we to suppose that she kept some large, sharp-pointed instrument se ted about her person, on the off-chance that she could get hold of Peter's Aqua-Lung and damage it?"

Mr. Trubody smoothed his neat mustache. He was shocked, but not incapable of judging a proposition on its merits.

"What could Peter expect to get out of such a—such an extraordinary trick?"

"Well, perhaps he hoped it would produce a showdown between Miss Ambrose and yourself."

"I don't follow you."

"He believes, rightly or wrongly, that she was responsible for your daughter's trouble at school and for the brain fever which resulted from it. He believes Miss Ambrose persecuted Faith. It is possible—I don't say it's the truth—that Peter has decided to persecute Miss Ambrose back."

"Oh, come, come! Boyish pranks, yes; but not cold-blooded vindictiveness like that."

"Well, of course, you know Peter best. But he passionately wants his sister's name cleared, as he puts it. It may be that he thinks, if he could break Miss Ambrose down, she could be made to confess that her accusations against Faith were false. That's what I meant by persecution campaign."

There was a silence. Mr. Trubody fiddled with his gold cigarette case, took out a cigarette, stared at it, put it back. He was seeking, Nigel guessed, to adjust his mind to the idea of Peter as a Vindice—the seventeen-year-old, conventional, rather pompous house prefect, the clean-limbed, clean-living son, playing about in such muddy waters.

"How do you come into this?" he asked at last.

"I don't think it would do anyone any good—not even Peter and Faith—if Miss Ambrose were pushed over the edge."

"No," said Mr. Trubody after another pause. "I simply cannot credit it. I've always found Peter a responsible boy. Mind you, he is reckless physically. But just now he's at the stage of taking himself very seriously—well, a bit self-important and priggish. I can't see him acting in such a *childish* way; he'd think it beneath his dignity."

"Perhaps it's the sea air."

Mr. Trubody frowned at what seemed to him a flippancy.

"Cruise life," continued Nigel, "does breed irresponsibility. Look at all the shipboard 'romances.' And it's easy for boys of seventeen to regress into childishness, particularly when they have an overdose of responsibility at school. It's kind of compensation."

"You may be right," said Mr. Trubody briskly, with the air of closing a business conference. "I'll keep an eye on the boy. Talking of shipboard romances, Peter's a bit sweet on the sister, have you noticed? Well, calf love won't do him any harm. Attractive woman. Perhaps she'll put all this nonsense about Miss Ambrose out of his head."

Yes, thought Nigel, it's all very easy and civilized; but, like a good many business high-ups, you haven't much time for personal moral problems.

III

Clare and Nigel sat outside a little café facing the harbor, with glasses of ouzo and iced water on the table. The whole population of Kalymnos, it seemed, had turned out to inspect the visitors. A handsome boy, carrying a tray of cakes, stopped at their table, was driven away by the café proprietor, and soon drifted back. Nigel bought some cakes; then Clare took out her sketchbook and began a quick sketch of the boy. A crowd of children instantly collected, were dispersed by one of the Tourist Police, and reassembled as soon as he had moved on. Barefoot, swarthy, ragged, they had enough vitality to power a factory; the girls tended to group themselves at a little distance, giggling or staring pertinaciously at Nigel: the boys were bolder; they crowded around Clare, breathing down her neck, yelling encouragement to the cake boy, who struck a variety of attitudes in front of Clare.

Presently she took out the leaf and presented her sketch to him. He held it in both hands, with a natural reverence that she found most moving; then selected four more cakes and gave them to her, his face positively floodlit with pleasure and pride.

A larger, sullen-looking boy, who had been standing nearby but dissociating himself from the general fraternization, now moved away.

"Do not mind him. He is political. Communist," said the cake boy.

"You speak English, then."

"I learn. In school."

"You will go to America?"

"No. I stay here. My father is the most good baker in Kalymnos. Then I shall be the most good."

After they had been chatting a while, the sullen-looking boy returned, with a small octopus writhing around his hand and wrist. He bashed the octopus many times on the cobbles. Clare was about to protest, but the cake boy said: "Make more soft. More good to eat."

The sullen boy, throwing back his hair and smiling cautiously at Clare, offered her the octopus. She accepted it with every appearance of delight. After a tactful interval, Nigel gave the boy a fifty-drachma note. He stared at it: astonishment, suspicion, greed, and pride chased one another over his face. Then he beamed from ear to ear, and suddenly raced off with the note as if he had stolen it. The mob of children, yelling, pursued him; two of them, in sheer excess of emotion, hurled themselves off the quayside into the sea.

"What on earth am I to do with this octopus?" asked Clare desperately. "It's not dead yet."

"Eat it alive, darling."

"I don't even like them cooked. It's like eating strips of rubber ball. Hello, isn't that Nikki?"

The children having dispersed, they could see right along the quayside to the harbor offices near which they had disembarked. The square-shouldered figure of the cruise manager was moving away from them, a hundred yards off. He was alone. He glanced around once or twice;

and his gait was that of a man who, without actually walk-ing on tiptoe, seeks not to attract attention. He kept close to the walls of the white and blue houses, walking in their shadow, and in a moment was lost to view.

"Tomcat on the prowl," said Clare lazily. "He's after your glamorous brunette, bet you anything."

"She's not my—what makes you think that?"

"I espied them on the sun deck after breakfast. Nikki was pointing out the landscape to Melissa. He was pointing away to the left of the harbor—the direction he's walking in now."

"Oh well, good luck to him. But," he added, echoing Clare's own thought, "how will they ditch Ianthe?"

"You're looking very handsome, love," said Clare. "In your dilapidated way."

Nigel gazed back at her. The black waterfall of hair pour-ing over her shoulders; the skin, white and lustrous as mag-nolia flowers, which the sun had hardly touched; the deep, dark, velvety eyes; the pale-rose-colored mouth. He seemed to be seeing Clare for the first time. How many times she had made him see her for the first time!

"Yes?" he said.

"Yes." She was breathing a little faster, and the blood faintly mantled her pale skin.

"Shall we go back to the ship?"

"No. I want the sun on me. You and the sun."

"Let's explore the island, then."

"Let's explore the island."

IV

"What are you afraid of?" said Faith Trubody. She was trembling all over, herself.

"You, my dear. And myself." Jeremy Street cast an un-easy look around him. The hillside fell away at their feet, stony and empty. There was no wind off the sea. The pine trees overhead did not even whisper. It was early afternoon.

"Don't you understand? I love you," the girl said, intensely, almost angrily.

"You're very sweet, Faith. And very young."

"I'm seventeen."

"And I'm nearly three times your age."

"What does age matter?" The girl's voice was fierce, and her irregular teeth showed.

"You look like a fierce little snarling fox."

Faith shivered again. "When you talk to me, it makes me tremble, like the pedal notes of an organ. I can't help it."

An expression of weariness came over the man's face. These yearning females and their pathetic, pseudoliterary talk.

"Look, Faith, you're a child still. Your father trusts me."

"Damn my father! And if you tell me I'm a child again, I'll hit you. But I suppose you get dozens of women throwing themselves at your head."

"Good gracious, no! I'm a back number now." For once there was a trace of real emotion in Jeremy Street's voice —the emotion of self-pity.

"You a back number! But everyone thinks you're wonderful—your lectures, your books. Everyone," she added, with the fatal honesty of youth, "everyone but the Bross."

The schoolgirl nickname irritated Jeremy. Another wave of depression, deadly as a nausea, swept through him. He thought of his expensive tastes, and his dwindling private income; the sales of his books declining; the slackening demand for his services as a lecturer. The slump had started, or so he had convinced himself, when Miss Ambrose began to attack him in the *Journal of Classical Studies,* three years ago.

She was like a corrosive acid eating away at his pride and his pocket. His antipathy to this woman had been accumulating for a long time, poisoning his system all the more because his vanity prevented him from revealing to anyone how deeply she wounded him. All his fear of failure was now focused upon Ianthe Ambrose; resentment had deepened into hatred, and might soon become a monomania. The public humiliation she had inflicted on him after his last lecture kept nagging at him like a chronic heartburn.

"What are you thinking about?" asked Faith.

"Miss Ambrose."

"Oh, you don't have to worry about her. She's just a sour old Lesbian."

"I'm not worrying about her," the man irritably replied. "But she's a public nuisance."

"I hate her too, actually."

Jeremy looked down at the girl who lay beside him. His exasperation with Ianthe, and his unadmitted fear of her, were suddenly transferred to an easier prey. Dragging Faith into his lap, he began to kiss her violently, as if releasing on the girl a pent-up fury. She went rigid, her sharp teeth locked together in a kind of rictus; then, softening, she flung her arms around his neck.

Presently, leaning back against Jeremy's shoulder, she said, "So it's like that."

"Like what?" he muttered.

"Hard. Cruel. As if you hated me."

"I ought to hate myself for it."

Faith shook her blond head impatiently. For all her infatuation, she could recognize insincerity now when she heard it.

"Hate yourself? Just for kissing me? Don't be silly."

The slight contempt in her voice pricked his vanity. He pushed her down, and had begun to go further than kissing when a flash of light along the hillside, a hundred yards away, caught his eye.

"What's that?"

"Go on! Make love to me!" The girl's eyes were shut.

"I think someone may be watching us. Binoculars. I saw a flash."

"Oh, damn!"

The childish crudity of it made him wince with distaste. He drew back from the flushed, tousled girl. But, if they had been observed, it would be all up with him. Mr. Trubody was an influential man.

"Your father would go up in smoke, wouldn't he?"

"Daddy? Why should he know about it?"

"I mean, if I told him I wanted to marry you."

"Marry me?" Faith sat bolt upright, her face averted. Oh God, thought Jeremy, she's going to say "Goody!"

"Oh no, Jeremy. That's quite different. I don't want to *marry* you. I don't want to marry anyone yet."

"Well, what the devil—?"

"I'm mad about you, of course. But I want experience."

"Oh, I see," he said, bitterly confounded. "I was to give an elementary course in sex? That was your idea? Well, you certainly need one."

Faith smiled secretly. She was tasting for the first time her woman's power, and she liked the taste. Her green eyes looked into his, not shyly now. "You do want me," she said.

"I don't want that person with binoculars to go rushing off to your father and tell him I was trying to seduce you."

"Yes. That would be a bit awkward."

"Awkward!" Jeremy Street's mind was a confusion of feelings; but soon they all slipped into the deep, familiar groove and went whirling around there. Ianthe Ambrose was responsible for this new predicament, too. If Ianthe's hostility had not become an obsession with him, he would never have got into this false position with Faith. Somehow, Ianthe must be silenced. And there was Mr. Trubody. Money and influence. Jeremy had been making up to the Trubodys during the cruise, with the plan of diverting some of the Trubody wealth into a cultural project from which he would himself largely benefit. He had harped on the theme of Big Business as patron of the arts, and laid himself out to impress Mr. Trubody. But Ianthe's performance at his last lecture must have undone all his good work. To marry Faith—and of course, he managed to persuade himself now, he had never intended it as a serious proposal —would have been a desperate expedient indeed. And tonight, before the dance, he had to lecture again; his last chance, maybe, to re-establish himself in Mr. Trubody's shrewd eyes as a worthy candidate for patronage. Yes, Ianthe Ambrose must be dealt with, and quickly.

He looked at his watch, got to his feet abruptly, shouldered the haversack in which they had brought their picnic lunch.

"I've got to be off," he said, not looking at the girl. Even in his present state of mind, he was piqued because she made no attempt to delay him.

He set off down the hillside. Faith lay back under the pines, a little, sharp smile on her face—a look, almost, of gloating. There was the same expression on the face of the man who now, unobserved by Faith, detached himself from behind the boulder, a hundred yards away, and, with his camera slung around his neck, followed Jeremy Street down toward the harbor.

V

Later that afternoon, Primrose Chalmers and her parents were plodding along the dusty track that led westward from the port. They had visited a Venetian castro in the hills during the morning, had a picnic and a siesta, and were now in search of a place to bathe.

About a mile from the little town, the winding track turned to the right around an escarpment, and a deep cove was disclosed. On the far side of the cove there was a tumble of rocks, and above them the track disappeared around another escarpment. Among these rocks two women were sitting. The bright-yellow bathing cap of Melissa Blaydon showed like lichen against a gray-black boulder.

The Chalmerses rounded the inlet, and from the road above hailed the two women.

"Hallo! What a marvelous spot you've found for a bathe. May we share it with you?"

"It's no good," called Ianthe Ambrose, who had got to her feet. "Absolutely black with sea urchins. We're just sunbathing."

There was a safe beach, she added, half a mile further on.

"That's got rid of them," she said to Melissa when the Chalmerses had padded off around the escarpment. "I couldn't face an afternoon of that abominable child."

"Do you suppose there really are sea urchins there?" the abominable child was saying to her parents. "Or does she want to hog it all for herself?"

"Well, Nikki did warn us that we ought to go to one of the regular bathing beaches."

"The water looked lovely and deep there. I bet Nikki told Mrs. Blaydon about it privately, so she could wallow all by herself."

"Come now, Primrose. That's not a very disinterested remark, is it?" said her mother mildly.

"Nikki's not a very disinterested man, where Mrs. Blaydon is concerned," the child replied in dogmatic tones.

"It is unwise, Primrose," her father stated, "to oversimplify any problem which stems from sexuality." He developed his theme, Primrose trailing beside him, her lower lip stuck out, till the track brought them to a strip of concrete paving, a few abandoned huts, and a small, stony beach below them.

It was not a very appetizing spot for a bathe, but at least there were no rocks immediately visible and therefore no sea urchins.

Primrose splashed about for a little, in a preoccupied way, then put on her clothes again and left her parents, who were discussing Melanie Klein's findings on the significance of the Inability to Mourn. She went half a mile back along the rough road, having researches of her own to pursue, and was presently peering around the escarpment which jutted out above the western side of the cove.

Curiosity had brought her thus far, fear held her back

Annihilation 79

from approaching any nearer. She wished to prove her theory that the cove was really a safe, an ideal place for bathing, but she had a healthy respect for Miss Ambrose's tongue—the teachers at her own progressive school had never, even under the greatest provocation, spoken to her as Miss Ambrose did. It would be gratifying, reflected Primrose, to prove that Miss Ambrose had lied about the presence of sea urchins.

Unfortunately, the steep, bouldered slope between the track and the sea concealed from her, as she peered around the escarpment, the spot where the two sisters had been sunbathing. She thought of climbing higher up the escarpment, so that she might overlook them. But at this moment her eye was caught by an object gradually floating out into view from under the overhang of the rocks. From its shape and color, she deduced what this object must be—her sight was not good enough to descry it clearly. For a few minutes, nothing more happened. Then there came a splashing sound, and the dark sleek head of a swimmer appeared; the swimmer retrieved the object which had floated out from shore, and swam back out of Primrose's view again.

The child left her point of vantage, and, returning to the beach where her parents were still talking, took out the notebook and pen from her sporran. The pen, she discovered, had run dry. So she borrowed a pencil from her father, sat down at a little distance, and wrote up her recent observations. Her tongue stuck out at one side of her mouth as she made her notes. She felt pleased with herself. Miss Ambrose *had* lied. Lied, it was possible, not only about the sea urchins, but . . .

Primrose put away the notebook and began to think up a plan.

Half an hour later the Chalmers family started back for the harbor. The sun was declining toward the west, so that the nearer side of the cove, as they approached it, was now in shadow. They rounded the promontory. Among the rocks on the cove's opposite shore, in full sunlight, sat a woman wearing a bathrobe. She waved to them. As they came nearer and saw it was Melissa, she draped a towel around her head: the yellow bathing cap, her bikini, and her dress were spread out on a rock, the wicker case lay beside her.

"Did you bathe after all, Mrs. Blaydon?" said Mrs. Chalmers.

"Yes. It's all right this side. I'm afraid my sister was fussing."

"Well, don't be late. The *Menelaos* leaves in three-quarters of an hour, you know," said Mr. Chalmers, looking down at Melissa from the track.

"I won't."

"Where's Miss Ambrose?" asked Primrose.

"She went on ahead. You may catch up with her."

They did not, however, see Ianthe Ambrose on their way back to the harbor. At the quayside there was a group of passengers, waiting for the next boat to take them back to the *Menelaos.* Mrs. Hale carried a huge sponge in her string bag. On a bollard, apart from the others, sat Peter Trubody. He was staring at nothing in particular—or perhaps at some picture in his own mind; the boy's eyes had such a haunted, sick look, his whole attitude was so dejected, that Mr. Chalmers asked him if he was feeling all right.

"Why shouldn't I be? You're the third person who—for God's sake leave me alone!" Peter ungraciously muttered.

The boy, said Mr. Chalmers to himself, has had a traumatic experience.

VI

"Oh dear, I am sleepy," yawned Clare. "And it's only six o'clock."

"I'm not surprised. Considering—" Nigel's words were cut off by a third bellow from the *Menelaos'* steam whistle, followed by an outbreak of shouting and gesticulation from the sailors who were about to haul up the gangway. A boat was putting out from the harbor, a man standing up in the bows waving frenziedly. When it drew alongside, the caique was seen to contain three boatmen, a mob of children, Peter Trubody, and Melissa Blaydon.

Nigel watched a sailor go down the gangway and help her out. She was limping heavily. Her face was half concealed by a headscarf.

"I turned my ankle on the way back. Awfully stupid of me. These damned roads of yours!" she said to Nikki, who was standing with a solicitous expression at the head of the gangway.

"I'll tell Dr. Plunket to come to your cabin."

"No, no, certainly not, Nikki. It doesn't need that sort of treatment," she added, in a low voice, giving the cruise manager a deep look.

Rummaging in her bag, she handed her landing card to the smart, white-uniformed quartermaster who waited nearby, thanked Peter for his escort, and hobbled off, carrying her wicker case, toward her cabin.

"So they did," was Clare's comment.

"Who did what?" asked Nigel.

"Melissa and Nikki managed to get rid of Ianthe. I must say they're rather overdoing the circumspection, though."

"Circumspection?"

"Oh, coming back on different caiques. And Melissa pretending she's turned her ankle to explain why she's so late. She'd jump at the chance of a handsome doctor fondling her tiny foot, if there was anything really wrong with it."

"Puss, puss," said Nigel; but he remembered Melissa, on Delos, arching a pretty foot for him to put on her shoe. "I expect Nikki has to be careful. Might lose his job if there were complaints that he was carrying on with female passengers."

"The only thing I have against cruise life," said Clare, yawning again, "is that it's turning us all into busybodies and gossips."

Certainly, rumor flies faster and more erratically on shipboard than anywhere else. An hour later, at dinner, Mrs. Hale was able to inform Clare authoritatively that Ianthe Ambrose had returned to the ship in the middle of the afternoon with sunstroke, and was keeping to her cabin but refusing the services of the doctor. Jeremy Street, she added, must be pleased; he would be spared the attentions of Miss Ambrose when he lectured tonight; it was a clear example of good coming out of evil.

"And so," Mrs. Hale added, "is Kalymnos. A horrid, stony place; nothing but urchins—sea and land ones. But out of it came *this.*" She reached down under her chair and fetched up a monster sponge, which she placed on the table for them to admire.

"My wife can't be parted from it," said the Bishop. "She carries it about everywhere, like a guilty conscience."

"No shop, *please*, dear. We're on holiday. Here's Mrs. Blaydon."

The woman approached their table, bearing a plate of fruit. She was wearing the Indian shawl over her head; it framed her beautiful face in an oval of brilliant color. As she went past, Mrs. Hale said:

"I hope your sister will soon be better."

"Oh, it was only a little touch of the sun, thank you. I'm taking her some fruit. She's determined to get up presently and attend the lecture."

When she had passed on, Mrs. Hale said, "More trouble in store for Mr. Street, I fear. What a lot of make-up the Merry Widow has put on tonight."

"Her complexion has to compete with that Indian shawl," Clare said.

"And with yours, my dear, at the dance."

"But she won't be able to dance, with that limp," said the Bishop.

"She'll be able to sit out, though," his wife replied, her brown eyes bright with mischief.

"You would never suppose," the Bishop remarked to Clare and Nigel, "that my wife is really one of the kindest-hearted women in the world, when anyone's in trouble."

Mrs. Hale flushed at the praise and the implicit, gentle rebuke.

The dance was due to begin at 9:30 P.M. in the big lounge forward. Jeremy Street's talk, which would be given on the boat deck aft, was timed for nine to nine-thirty. The chairs in the lounge had been pushed back against the walls, and the three Greek musicians were warming up with bouzouki songs. Sitting with Clare on a window seat beneath one of the windows which overlooked the fo'c's'le of the *Menelaos,* Nigel listened to the virile, infectious tunes and decided he would not attend the lecture. He noticed Melissa Blaydon at the bar, and how the musicians were conscious of her presence there. The Trubodys sat in a group on the opposite side of the lounge. Jeremy Street, for once, was not with them; Peter eyed Melissa Blaydon across the room with an expression which Nigel found disquieting.

Presently Melissa left the lounge. The music seemed to lose a little of its sparkle. Peter Trubody stared morosely in front of him. About ten minutes later, the lounge cleared a bit as passengers went out to the lecture. The ship was rolling now. A wind had been getting up, and on the exposed boat deck Jeremy Street would have a job making himself heard. Some of the windows being open, the thump and swish of waves made an accompaniment to the staccato Greek music.

"Nigel, do shut that window. My hair is being blown all over the place," said Clare, after they had been listening for a while. The musicians had just finished another song. Nigel knelt on the window seat. He was winding up the window when, amidst the rushing noise of the sea, he heard a faint scream and a splash. Ten seconds later, perhaps, the sounds were repeated. There were people larking about still in the ship's swimming pool. Nigel looked out; but the canopy over the pool prevented him from seeing anything. Late for a bathe, he thought, automatically looking at his watch, which said 9:13. He finished winding up the window.

About ten minutes later, Nikki came into the lounge. He spoke briefly to the band, looked around to make sure that everything was ready for the dance, flashed his teeth at Clare. But all this was done, Nigel vaguely felt, without his usual brio; Nikki seemed—was it preoccupied, a little unsure of himself, puzzled?

There was no time to speculate on this. The lounge started to fill up again. Trade at the bar was brisk. The musicians, refreshed with ouzo, took up their position and began retuning the violin and guitar to the piano.

Ivor Bentinck-Jones, who wore a dreadful Palm Beach shirt, was in his element, fussing to and fro between the musicians, the more distinguished passengers, and Nikki. As Clare remarked, he was one of Nature's masters of ceremonies.

The dance began soon after nine-thirty. During the second foxtrot, Clare said to Nigel, "My word, Melissa's dressed to kill. Look!" The woman was indeed a breathtaking sight as she made her entrance, in a gold and crimson sari. Limping to the bar, she ordered brandy and sat on a high stool, smiling remotely and mysteriously around her.

It was during a lull, while Ivor Bentinck-Jones was trying to organize a Highland Reel and convey its rhythm to the musicians ("the man's never been nearer Scotland than the end of a whisky bottle," remarked Mrs. Hale), that Nigel noticed Mr. and Mrs. Chalmers enter the lounge, look anxiously around it, then withdraw again. Ten minutes later, they were back. Mr. Chalmers took Nikki aside. The cruise manager, waiting till the musicians had finished their number, went to the public-address system, which broadcast throughout the ship.

"I have a message for Primrose Chalmers. Will Primrose Chalmers come at once to the main lounge forward. Her parents are waiting for her there."

The dance was resumed. Nigel, going across to get a drink for Clare, found Peter Trubody at the bar.

"You look absolutely marvelous in that dress, Mrs. Blaydon," the boy was saying in a low, intense voice.

"Thank you, sir."

"What have you got on your hair?"

"It's perfumed oil I spray on it," she answered, rearranging with a delicate gesture the sari, which had slipped back a little on her head, revealing the dark, wet shine of her hair.

"Jolly bad luck you can't dance tonight," said the boy. "I'd have loved a dance with you."

"Next time, Peter."

Nikki was in earnest conversation with the first officer, a smart young man in white uniform with blue and gold epaulets. Nigel brought Clare her drink. Nikki took up the microphone and broadcast again the message for Primrose Chalmers. The dancing continued, but it was halfhearted now—some premonition seemed to cast its shadow over the revelers, in spite of Mr. Bentinck-Jones's efforts to whoop things up.

When, after the second broadcast failed to elicit Primrose, Nigel gravitated toward the little group near the doors of the lounge, he found Bentinck-Jones at his elbow. Nikki was telling the Chalmerses that he would institute a search of the ship. They themselves had looked everywhere for their daughter, who had slipped away before the lecture was over and not been seen by them since. It was long past her bedtime now, said Mrs. Chalmers.

Nikki spoke to the first officer. As the latter was about to move off, Nigel drew Nikki out of earshot of the parents.

"Tell them not to omit the swimming pool in their search."

The cruise manager stared at Nigel with astonishment and a trace of suspicion. However, he spoke again, in rapid, staccato language, to the first officer.

Nikki's anxiety, evident now, was contagious. The dancing petered out, and the passengers stood about uneasily or went on deck. Nigel meditated on the impulse which had made him suggest the swimming pool: a couple of faint screams, a couple of splashes—it was all odds that, as he'd assumed at the time, people had just been larking about there.

It seemed to take a long time to search a ship. There were, perhaps, seventy cabins; the kitchens; the engine room; the ship's boats—the child might have gone to sleep in one of them, or she could have fallen overboard, the way the *Menelaos* had been rolling.

More than half an hour later, Nikki entered the lounge and beckoned to the red-haired Dr. Plunket. Nigel followed them forward along the promenade deck onto the fo'c's'le. The first officer was there; and two sailors—one of them dripping wet; but not, for once, the ubiquitous Ivor Bentinck-Jones. Stretched on the iron deck lay the body of the child Primrose. She was fully clothed, including the sporran.

"My God, this is terrible," exclaimed Nikki. "An accident, on the first of our cruises. What will the directors say? Are you sure she's dead, doctor?"

On his knees beside the body, Dr. Plunket looked up. "She's dead all right. But it was not an accident." He pointed to the child's throat where, in the light of the arc lamp slung from the forestay, hideous bruises were visible. "Strangled, and then flung into the pool, I'd say."

The cruise manager was looking half demented. "How am I to tell this poor child's mother—?"

"Nikki," said Nigel sharply. "Go and find Mrs. Hale—you know, the Bishop of Solway's wife. Tell her what has happened. Ask her to break it to the child's parents."

"Yes, yes. Sure thing. A most suitable idea. I go."

Nikki went. From the lounge above came sounds of music. The band was trying to get some revelry going again.

"Ought to be 'Nearer, My God, to Thee,' eh?" said Dr. Plunket dryly.

"Will you just look in her sporran, doctor," said Nigel urgently. "Is there a notebook there?"

"No. A handkerchief, a pencil, a pen, a miniature golliwog," said the doctor, as he laid these articles on the deck beside the body. "No notebook. What's the idea? We shouldn't be touching anything till the police—damn it, I was forgetting where we are."

"The police *are* here, more or less."

"What the devil—?"

Nigel spoke rapidly for a minute or two. The Greek sailors gazed at him curiously; one of them picked up the miniature golliwog, stroked its woolly head, and put it down again.

"I see," said Dr. Plunket. "So that's who I've been harboring in my cabin. Well, you've got a hell of a job before you."

How much of a job, Nigel realized ten minutes later. The first officer had arrived with two more sailors, bearing a stretcher. Primrose's body had been taken away to her cabin. The rumor had flown around, and passengers were flocking toward the fo'c's'le. Dr. Plunket pushed his way against the tide of them, following the stretcher. Nigel went to look for Clare in the lounge.

As he entered, he saw Nikki, like a figure in a recurrent nightmare, go to the public-address system. Nikki was sweating; his swarthy complexion had paled to a muddy yellow, and his voice was barely under control. Taking up the microphone, he said:

"I have a message for Miss Ambrose. Miss Ianthe Ambrose. Will Miss Ambrose go at once to her cabin, where her sister is awaiting her. Will any passenger who has seen Miss Ambrose since the lecture this evening, come to the forward lounge, promenade deck, and inform me. This is the cruise manager speaking."

Investigation

LISTING HEAVILY to starboard, the *Menelaos* turned in her
tracks. Her searchlight scythed an arc across the sea; on the
bridge and in the bows, sailors were looking out. It had to
be done, but the ship's officers knew the search was futile.
Ianthe Ambrose could have gone overboard any time after
9:10, when she was seen to leave the lecture, and on her
own statement she had been no swimmer.

It was now nearly two in the morning. The Captain ges-
tured to the second officer, who went out into the wheelhouse. The telegraph clanged; the *Menelaos*, which had
steamed some way back toward Kalymnos in the crisscross
search, now put about and at full speed set her course
westward to Athens. The Captain had been in communication with his owners by radio-telephone, and they had in-
structed him to use his own discretion about the length of
the search, then to break off the cruise and return to

Athens direct. There, it would be a matter for the Greek police and the British Embassy to sort out.

Nigel Strangeways, who had shown his credentials to the Captain, and been given leave to conduct a preliminary semiofficial investigation, was now sitting in the Captain's cabin. There were also present the cruise manager, Dr. Plunket, and the first officer. The Captain, a gray-haired man with a hooked nose and a brusque manner, motioned Nigel to begin; he understood a certain amount of English, but now and then asked Nikki to interpret.

"I'll give you the facts first, gentlemen," said Nigel. "Mr. Chalmers attended the lecture with his wife and daughter. Miss Ambrose was sitting at the end of the row in front of them. He noticed that she was in a very depressed state of mind; she sat huddled up, her face in her hands, and occasionally she muttered or moaned to herself. Mr. Chalmers thought that the muttering and moaning were by way of being a protest against the lecture—she took a dim view of Mr. Street's abilities—"

" 'Dim view'?" asked the Captain.

"Sorry. She thought he was a charlatan, no good at his job."

"But Mr. Street is a most famous—" Nikki began to protest. The gray-haired captain cut him short with a slicing movement of the hand.

"The lecture began punctually at 9 P.M. About ten minutes after it had started Mr. Chalmers heard Miss Ambrose give a loud sigh. Then she got up and walked away. Several other passengers corroborate this. Primrose Chalmers, who was sitting at the end of her row, *may* have slipped out immediately after Miss Ambrose. Her parents did not notice she was gone till a minute or two later, and I haven't yet found any eyewitnesses of her departure—it's pretty dark up on the boat deck at that time, and the audience were very attentive—Mr. Street was in particularly good form, it seems. Well now, Miss Ambrose left the lecture at approximately 9:10, and Primrose between 9:10 and 9:12."

"You're thinking there was some collusion between them?" asked the red-haired Dr. Plunket.

"'Collusion'?" said the Captain.

"Not collusion," said Nigel. "Some *connection* between Miss Ambrose's leaving and Primrose's leaving. At 9:13, while I was sitting by an open window in the main lounge, above the swimming pool, I heard a faint cry and a splash. About ten seconds later these sounds were repeated. I looked out, but I couldn't see anything—the canopy over the swimming pool was still in position."

The Captain spoke rapidly to the first officer. Nigel guessed he was asking why the hell, in view of the stiff wind that was blowing then, the canopy had not been taken down.

"I assumed some passengers were playing about down there. However, when I heard Primrose was missing, I advised Nikki to have the swimming pool searched. Her body, as you know, was found floating a little way below the surface. We have no proof yet that she was killed immediately after leaving the lecture. We must inquire tomorrow if anyone saw her between that time and the time her body was discovered, and if any other passengers *were* in the swimming pool at 9:13."

The Captain, eying Nigel keenly, nodded approval.

"Let us assume for the moment," Nigel continued, "that the sounds I heard were made by Primrose and her murderer. How do we interpret them, *two* cries and *two* splashes, at an interval of ten seconds?"

"Until they do an autopsy at Athens," put in Dr. Plunket, "we can't tell for certain whether she was strangled in the pool or strangled outside it and then thrown in. But the fact that the body was found just below the surface strongly suggests the former. If she screamed as she fell or was thrown into the pool, her mouth would be open and she'd take enough water into her lungs for the body to sink a little; her wet clothing also would tend to pull her down. But if she was strangled outside the pool, and thrown into it dead, one would expect the body to remain on the surface for a day or two."

He spoke fast, and Nikki was required by the Captain to translate. While he did so, Nigel saw in his mind's eye the unsightly body of Primrose, packed among those giant cubes of ice he had watched being taken aboard at the Piraeus, and stored somewhere in the hold, with other meat.

"You were talking about the sounds," said the Captain.

"Yes. *Two* splashes. Did the murderer strangle Primrose on the edge, throw her in, see she was not quite dead, and jump in himself to finish the job? Did the child manage to scramble out of the pool after the first attack, and have to be thrown back into it? And these are not the only possibilities."

"I do not think this is important," said the Captain.

"It *may* be important, in deciding whether the murderer was Miss Ambrose herself."

Nikki's brown eyes bulged. "Oh, but surely she committed suicide—threw herself overboard?"

"She might have done that after killing Primrose."

"Or *because* she had killed her?" suggested the doctor.

"The point is this," said Nigel. "Miss Ambrose could not swim, or always said she couldn't. The water in the swimming pool is kept at a level of about five and a half feet. Miss Ambrose was rather less than that in height. So she could hardly strangle the child *in* the pool. But, if she strangled her on the deck, what was the second splash?"

"You heard two cries," said the Captain in his slow English. "Of a man, or a woman?"

"I can't be sure. I'd say they were female. Or a boy's. But the wind was blowing too hard. What is inconceivable is that the child's death and Miss Ambrose's disappearance, within an hour of each other, should be unconnected. Miss Ambrose had been in a suicidal frame of mind—there's plenty of evidence for that. But she has left no suicide note" (Nikki translated this for the Captain) "and she went to the lecture; you don't go to a lecture if you're just about to kill yourself."

"Suicides do some damned queer things; but I'm inclined to agree," said Dr. Plunket.

"You have a theory?" Nikki asked.

"Several people on board had fairly strong motives for killing Ianthe Ambrose. And, since she was obviously unbalanced, a murderer could calculate that her disappearance, when he pitched her overboard, would be put down as suicide. The obvious theory is that Primrose saw him throwing Ianthe off the ship, and had to be silenced."

"But you do not think it happens so?" said the Captain. He went off into a Sten-gun burst of Greek, which Nikki translated—

"The Captain says, have you ever tried to throw a full-grown woman over the rail of a ship? Also, there were many people on deck."

"Tell the Captain I haven't, but the fo'c's'le is little used by passengers unless they're bathing in the pool."

When Nikki had translated, Nigel went on, "There is an alternative theory—that the murderer's object was to kill Primrose, that Ianthe saw him doing it, and so he had to silence her."

"But why not strangle Ianthe and push her into the swimming pool too?" asked Dr. Plunket.

"Why should anyone want to hurt a harmless kid like this Primrose Chalmers?" Nikki said.

"I don't know about 'harmless.' She pried about and eavesdropped among the passengers, and wrote it all down in a notebook. That notebook could be dynamite"—Nigel paused while Nikki translated—"and it has disappeared. She always kept it in her sporran—that leather pouch she wore over her skirt. The notebook was not in the sporran when Dr. Plunket examined the body. And Mr. Chalmers cannot find it anywhere in their cabin."

"But the chap wouldn't have to murder the kid to get

hold of the notebook," Dr. Plunket objected. "He could just take it from her."

"That depends. She'd still have the information in her head after the notebook had been taken."

"Well then, she *would* be dangerous to the murderer."

"Not necessarily."

"I don't get you," said Dr. Plunket.

"She'd only be dangerous to him if she realized the importance of her knowledge. Captain, I'd like a word with the sailors who found the body."

The Captain rattled out orders. The first officer left the cabin. A steward entered, carrying cups of Turkish coffee, and the Captain uncorked a bottle of brandy.

When the first officer returned with the two sailors, Nigel questioned them through Nikki. Their evidence proved interesting. They had searched the fo'c's'le, then one of them had gone into the swimming pool (they had left this to the last, Nigel surmised, because like so many sailors they disliked physical contact with the element from which they made their living). After dragging out the body, one of the sailors went to report to the first officer. The other was accosted by a passenger, who came through the doorway from the promenade deck. Closely questioned by Nigel, this sailor admitted that the passenger had distracted his attention from the body for a few moments, long enough, Nigel believed, to take the notebook. The sailor described the passenger as a short man with a fat face and an American shirt. It fitted well enough the appearance of Ivor Bentinck-Jones.

The passenger, replied the sailor to Nigel's final question, had not seemed especially disturbed when he saw the body.

"I'd like this man to identify the passenger straight away," said Nigel to the Captain, who made an assenting gesture. Nikki interposed with a rattle of Greek—he was pointing out, no doubt, that the owners would take a poor view of passengers being dragged out of their beds in the small hours and accused of robbing corpses; but the Captain overruled him.

Nigel turned to Dr. Plunket. "How is Mrs. Blaydon taking it?"

"Pretty hard. I had to give her a sedative. She's not in a condition to be questioned yet."

"That can wait. But I wish you'd do one thing for me. Look at her ankle. She sprained it or turned it or something. See if it needs attention."

Dr. Plunket stared at Nigel for a moment. "All right. You're the boss."

II

"This is an outrage!" exclaimed Ivor Bentinck-Jones. "By whose authority—?"

"The Captain's authority. I'm glad you agree that the murder of a child is an outrage," said Nigel calmly.

"What? What's that? She was murdered?"

"Strangled. You didn't notice the bruises on her throat when you were examining her body?"

"Examining?—I never examined her body."

"Too busy robbing it, were you?"

Bentinck-Jones's face went dead for a moment, before it resumed its expression of violent protest. "That sort of remark could get you into serious trouble," he said.

"It's just as well there's nobody else to hear it, then," Nigel replied, goading him.

Bentinck-Jones had been brought to the first officer's cabin, which the Captain had assigned to Nigel for interviews. The man had put on trousers and a jersey over his pajamas; his sparse hair stuck up in spikes, and he had forgotten to replace his false teeth. He no longer looked the life and soul of the party.

"If that's your line," he said coolly, "I demand that a witness be present at this interview."

"Are you sure that is wise? You don't mind a third person hearing about your, er, private activities?"

"No objection whatsoever."

Nigel's pale-blue eyes, at their chilliest now, scrutinized the man for several seconds.

"You do realize that you may be responsible for this child's death?" he asked.

"That's the most pernicious nonsense. And an actionable statement, too. I warn you—"

"Responsible for her death, I said. You spun her a yarn about being a Secret Service man looking for E.O.K.A. agents on board. It wouldn't deceive a child. It didn't deceive Primrose. But you had encouraged her to spy and eavesdrop among the passengers, and write it all down in her notebook. As a result, she discovered something which made her a menace to one of the passengers. Therefore she had to be killed."

"Well, *really!* I invent a little game, to amuse this child—"

"A useful game for you."

"I don't understand you."

"Her notebook would turn up, with any luck, some profitable openings for blackmail."

There was a silence. Ivor's mouth made a nibbling movement; his eyes were wary. Like all blackmailers, Nigel reflected, this man has iron nerves as well as a thick skin; let's see just how thick it is.

"You'd still like a witness?"

"I insist on one."

"Very well." Nigel opened the door, outside which stood an armed sailor, went to Nikki's cabin, and asked him to come along. As they entered, Nigel caught a flicker of—calculation, was it, or satisfaction?—on Bentinck-Jones's face.

"We were discussing blackmail," he told Nikki. Then, turning to Ivor, "We have cabled your description to Records at Scotland Yard. We shall get an answer this morning, if you are known there."

Bentinck-Jones sat back, his hands lightly clasped over his fat little stomach.

"You are accusing me of blackmail, before a witness? What evidence have you?"

"You started to blackmail me, for example. During our donkey trip on Mount Patmos."

"You're dreaming," Ivor protested. But a relief that he could not quite conceal showed in his face; it signified to Nigel that there was someone else on board in whom the man really had got his claws.

"Your methods," Nigel pursued, "are quite clever—in a third-rate way. Sly hints, delicate insinuations first, to try out the morale of a prospective victim. You're careful, at first, to say nothing which could not have an innocent interpretation. That's how you protect yourself. And then there's your double bluff—the professional blackmailer disguised as an amateur busybody—the real pest at work behind the harmless little nuisance. Quite a good camouflage."

Would that get through his skin, Nigel wondered. It did not seem to. The man's expression was complacent, almost contemptuous, as if these charges were too absurd to answer.

"On Patmos you talked to me about 'unmarried couples' in the context of Miss Massinger's possible commission to do a portrait bust of royalty. You were just probing, to discover my reactions. If I'd shown signs of perturbation—"

"Look at Nikki. He's as bewildered by this extraordinary rigmarole as I am."

Nigel kept his pale-blue eyes fastened on the man.

"Very well, then. We'll return to Primrose Chalmers. Have you any objection to your cabin and your person being searched—for her notebook?"

"None at all." Bentinck-Jones said it too quickly. Nigel realized with chagrin that the man must have disposed of the notebook he had taken off Primrose's body; he'd had four hours, after all, to master its contents. However, in the remote chance that Bentinck-Jones was bluffing, Nigel proceeded with the search. The notebook was not on him, nor in his cabin. Worse still, the man who shared the cabin with Ivor, and made no objection to his own belongings being searched too, said that Ivor had come into the cabin at about 11:15 and told him that the missing child had been found drowned; they had discussed it for a little, then turned out the lights. He himself had not been able to go to sleep, and could state definitely that Bentinck-Jones had not turned on the light or left the cabin till Nigel sent for him just now.

The body had been found just before 11 P.M. Ivor had turned up a minute or two later by the swimming pool. This would have given him less than a quarter of an hour to memorize the contents of the notebook, before pitching it overboard and returning to his cabin. Not long enough, surely?

And then, back in the first officer's cabin, with the contents of Primrose's sporran laid out on the table before him, Nigel realized with exasperation that all this was a dead end. He had seen the child taking notes, always with that fountain pen. The body had been in the water for the best part of two hours. The ink would have run, the writing become totally undecipherable.

He looked up sharply at Bentinck-Jones. The man's eyes were fixed upon the table where lay a handkerchief, a pencil, a miniature golliwog, and a pen. There was a faint smirk on his face.

"Tomorrow," said Nigel, "I shall be addressing the passengers. I shall tell them, without mentioning names, that there is a blackmailer on this cruise. I shall ask anyone who has been approached by this blackmailer to come to me privately. Whether the blackmailer's activities are linked with the murders of Primrose Chalmers and—"

"You could save your breath," said Ivor Bentinck-Jones, his fat voice grating now, "and ask this man what he was doing in Miss Ambrose's cabin at quarter-past nine last night."

Nigel turned his head. The cruise manager was staring at Ivor, an almost theatrical look of consternation on his face. "You accuse *me?* This is another of your lying black-mails! I—"

"Take it easy, Nikki."

"He is a liar!"

"No, you can't wriggle out of it." Ivor chuckled. "I happened to be following you along the passage, on my way to my cabin. You entered Miss Ambrose's—you should always knock, Nikki, before going into a lady's cabin. As I passed the door, I heard a struggle—"

"Stop! I can explain, I can—"

"About a minute later, you passed my own door, which happened to be ajar. You were breathing hard, your hair was rumpled, your tie halfway around your neck, and"—with an incredibly swift movement, Bentinck-Jones reached out and jerked up one of Nikki's sleeves—"yes, there were scratches on your wrists."

Nikki gave the man a bearlike clout, which sent him reeling. The armed sailor looked in, then shut the door again.

"You claim this happened at 9:15?" said Nigel, dancing the miniature golliwog on the table before him. "How do you remember the time so exactly?"

"I left the bar for a minute—the clock said just before 9:15—to come down and get a handkerchief. I came straight down."

And at 9:10 Ianthe Ambrose had left the lecture, said Nigel to himself.

"I will speak to Mr. Strangeways privately," said Nikki, glaring at Bentinck-Jones. "I will not speak before this filth, this grinning toad, this lousy heel of a—"

"Pipe down, Nikki. That'll be all for tonight, Bentinck-Jones. Thank you for your help."

"Watch your step, Strangeways. Just watch it. Good night."

III

"Well, Nikki?"

"You do not believe those lies, Mr. Strangeways? He is a blackmailer—you say so yourself—a criminal type."

"But they were not lies, Nikki, were they?"

The cruise manager's prune-dark eyes swiveled away; then, straightening his massive shoulders, he gave Nigel a rueful, a charming, an almost schoolboy look.

"No. They were not. But I did not kill anyone. I could not have killed Miss Ambrose."

"Why not?"

"Because it was Mel—her sister—in the cabin."

"You had an assignation with her, an arrangement to meet her there?"

"Sure thing. While her sister was at the lecture." Nikki opened his eyes wide, flashing his magnificent teeth at Nigel. "Oh boy! What a woman! This is private and confidential, yes?"

"We shall see."

"Women are crazy. You know? She says for me to come to her cabin, and when I go there she does not want it, she fights like a cat. It is their moods. They are crazy in their moods. And yet she had had a shower bath, and she was naked."

"Wait a minute, Nikki. Let's start at the beginning. When was this assignation made?"

"In the morning. Before we go ashore."

"To meet in her cabin, during the lecture?"

"O.K. correct."

Nigel remembered something Clare had told him. "You're sure the assignation was for her cabin, not for a bathing beach on the island?"

"I don't—oh, I get you; I did tell Mrs. Blaydon about a good place to bathe, where she could be private."

"You told her this as a favor?"

"Sure thing."

"You didn't plan to meet her there?"

"What'd be the use? Her sister was going to be with her."

"But Miss Ambrose returned alone to the ship in the middle of the afternoon."

"She did? Say, I guess I missed an opportunity, then," the cruise manager shamelessly remarked.

"*Did* you miss it? Miss Massinger and I saw you walking away in the direction of the cove."

A shutter came down over Nikki's eyes. "You must have been mistaken."

Nigel let it pass, for the time being, but noted the man's relief when he returned to the events of last night. Nikki had gone into Melissa Blaydon's cabin. It was quite dark. Melissa was there—"disrobed, undraped," said Nikki, airing his vocabulary with some complacence. She must have recently taken a shower, for her body was damp and her hair soaking. When she struggled with him, he thought at first she was just playing hard to get; but the violence of her reaction soon disabused him of this notion. "I am not one to take advantage of a lady when she is unwilling," he nobly remarked.

"But didn't she explain why she was unwilling?"

"No. She said nothing."

"*Nothing at all?* How very odd. You mean she didn't even cry out, or—?"

"She fought quite silently. She was stronger than I expected—very strong. I felt she was, well, sort of panicky, desperate. So I desisted from pressing my attentions upon her."

"Very gentlemanly of you, I'm sure. And afterward, during the dance, did she make any reference to what had happened?"

"I didn't speak to her during the dance. I was sore at her."

Nigel gazed meditatively at Nikki, who was made uncomfortable by it and lit a cigarette, turning his head away. Nigel's thoughts were not on the cruise manager, however;

he was thinking how peculiar it was that, just before the dance, a woman like Melissa should get her hair wringing wet. Surely, if she was taking a shower, she'd wear a bathing cap? And why had she said nothing, not a word of protest or explanation, to Nikki?

"What has all this to do with that poor child's being drowned?" the latter now asked.

"You get wet, drowning somebody," said Nigel, more to himself than to his companion. And Nikki had told him there was something "panicky, desperate" in the woman's resistance.

Nikki was looking a bit panicky himself. It might well lose him his job if this episode with Melissa came out. Or the panic might have a more sinister origin.

"How do these landing tickets work?" asked Nigel. "Are they checked every evening, after the passengers have re-embarked?"

"My secretary counts them, to see if there are the same number as we gave out in the morning. So we should know if a passenger had been left behind."

"And last night—did you have the right number?"

"Yes, sir. What's on your mind?" Nikki looked puzzled.

"Let us exercise pure reason, Nikki. Either Miss Ambrose was murdered, or she committed suicide. Take suicide first. She could, possibly, have thrown herself off the ship without being seen or heard. But did she strangle and drown Primrose Chalmers first? Why should she? Someone intent on killing herself doesn't take time off to kill somebody else *en route*. And anyway, the evidence points strongly to the child's having been strangled *in* the swimming pool. Ianthe, by all accounts, couldn't swim; therefore she could not have done it. What's the alternative?— that, within a short space of time, a woman commits suicide and a child is murdered, on the same ship, quite independently? Well, that'd be a fantastic coincidence. Take murder, then: Ianthe is murdered, possibly because she surprised the person who killed Primrose. It *looks* plausible. But Ianthe's body is not on the ship. Therefore, if she was murdered, she must have been thrown overboard. But the risk of doing so, with people strolling or sitting about on the decks all the time, would be appalling. And what was *she* supposed to be doing? If she saw someone kill Primrose, she'd yell for help, wouldn't she? Ditto if somebody laid hold on her to toss her overboard—she'd scream and struggle: it'd be a hell of a business, as the Captain said just now, to lift a full-grown, struggling woman over the rail."

"The killer might have stunned her first."

"He *might.* But, if she'd just seen him killing Primrose, do you think she'd have let him come near her? If she was not murdered because she witnessed that crime, you have to postulate two separate murderers operating independently at the same time, or else one murderer who wanted, for different reasons, to get rid of both Ianthe and Primrose, and found opportunities to do so on the same night."

"Ah, that's it!" Nikki enthusiastically exclaimed. "You've got something there! It is a privilege to watch British police methods at work. Pure reason! Divine reason!"

"No, no. It just won't do. Several people had motives for murdering Ianthe. But Primrose? A child with a notebook? She wasn't really such a menace. What could she have found out that would force anyone into killing her? Unless—" Nigel paused.

"Unless?"

"—she saw the murderer of Ianthe Ambrose. She did, after all, slip out of the lecture shortly after Ianthe." Nigel yawned and stretched. "Well, I'm for bed soon. Now: arrangements for tomorrow morning." . . .

IV

Immediately after breakfast, the English-speaking passengers were all assembled in the main dining saloon—all, with the exception of Melissa Blaydon and the Chalmerses. At one end, behind a table, sat the Captain of the *Menelaos,* flanked by Nigel and the cruise manager. The passengers muttered to one another, fidgeted, smoked, waiting for they did not quite know what to happen.

"What does this remind you of?" whispered Mrs. Hale to Clare Massinger.

"An extension lecture, in a café in a small Midland city," Clare promptly replied.

"The annual general meeting of a company that's going on the rocks," Mrs. Hale suggested. "I hope Mr. Strangeways will be able to handle the indignant shareholders."

Mr. Strangeways was saying to Dr. Plunket, who had just sat down beside him, "How is Mrs. Blaydon this morning?"

"A bit dopey still. But the natural Eve is indomitable. She'd made up her face for me. Vain woman; but attractive all right. Pulse normal, and—"

"Is her ankle normal?"

"How you do go on about her ankle. It's swollen—a slight sprain—nothing to worry about."

"When can I see her?"

"Midday perhaps. She was suffering from severe shock last night. Mustn't rush things."

A steward, standing by the door, made a sign to Nikki and put the passenger list under his arm. The cruise manager rose to his feet, radiating an aura of confidence edged with sorrow.

"The Captain has asked you to be present, ladies and gentlemen, and hopes you will all co-operate with Mr. Strangeways, to whom he has entrusted the preliminary investigation of the unfortunate occurrences which have—er—occurred on his ship."

"He's learned that bit off by heart," Mrs. Hale murmured in Clare's ear.

"Mr. Strangeways is connected with Scotland Yard," proceeded Nikki, giving a sudden beam like a conjuror producing the rabbit. There was a stir of interest among the passengers, many of whom craned their necks to view the hitherto incognito celebrity.

"You were right," whispered Mrs. Hale. "A lecture.

Nikki forgot to say that our distinguished speaker needs no introduction."

Nigel Strangeways was standing up now. The untidy, tow-colored hair, one lock hanging over his eye; the stoop; the furrowed face; the air of purposeful abstraction—all suggested a lecturer of the less orthodox academic type.

"I have no official standing," he began abruptly. "The Captain has asked me to do what I can. When we reach Athens, this affair will be in the hands of the Greek police. There's no sort of compulsion on any of you to answer my questions or co-operate with me in any way. However, the more we can get done before we reach Athens, the sooner we shall be able to resume our cruise. Nikki is making arrangements for the cruise to be continued, even if it has to be a curtailed itinerary. There's no reason"—Nigel's pale-blue eyes gazed non-committally at his audience—"there's no reason why the innocent should suffer with the guilty. So it will pay you to co-operate; it will pay all but one of you."

Nigel paused to light a cigarette, face crumpled, eyes screwed up. His last phrase, delivered in the same dry, forthright manner as the rest, had tautened the whole audience.

"Rather impressive," commented Mrs. Hale.

"He's a bit of an old show-off, really—can't resist a touch of drama," said Clare affectionately.

"Last night, as you all know by now, Primrose Chalmers was murdered, and Miss Ianthe Ambrose disappeared. The most convenient theory would be that Miss Ambrose strangled the child and then jumped overboard. But I fear we must not lay this flattering unction to our souls. For reasons I won't go into, the theory is barely tenable. In fact, it's almost certain that the murderer is on the ship still—probably sitting at one of these tables."

Nigel paused for the uneasy stir to subside.

"Miss Ambrose was last seen, so far as we know, leaving the lecture on the boat deck at about 9:10 P.M., and Primrose was missed by her parents two minutes later. The first information we need is this: did anyone here see either of them after 9:10? Some of you probably didn't know them, so we shall now hand around their passports with their photographs in them. The crew and the passengers of other nationalities have already been asked this question, with no result. While the passports are going around, will you please try to remember if you heard any suspicious sounds—those of you who were on or near the fo'c's'le where the swimming pool is—between 9:10 P.M. and the time when it was announced on the loud-speakers that Primrose was missing."

Nigel's questions produced one piece of evidence. Several passengers identified Miss Ambrose from the passport photograph as a woman they had seen walking along the promenade deck, from aft, at about the time in question. They had not particularly noticed her demeanor. One of the last passengers to look at the photo, a mousy woman with pince-nez, then rose to her feet, saying she had seen Primrose Chalmers catch up with Miss Ambrose on the promenade deck, just before the latter had reached the doorway leading in toward the forward saloon.

"What happened then?"

"The child took hold of Miss Ambrose's sleeve, as if to detain her. She spoke to Miss Ambrose—I couldn't hear what they were saying."

"This may be very important. Did Miss Ambrose seem surprised, impatient?"

"Well, I thought she went sort of stiff—I wasn't really paying much attention, though."

"Did they talk for long?"

"Oh no. In fact, I don't know if Miss Ambrose said anything. She tried—yes, I remember now—to pull her arm away, and I got the impression she wanted to go in off the deck—down to her cabin, I mean. But the child wouldn't let go, and said something more. Then they walked away, together, toward the front end of the ship. It all happened, oh, in half a minute, or less."

"Anything strike you about the way they walked off? Furtive, either of them?"

"It's funny you should say that, Mr. Strangeways. I remember thinking how quaint it was the little girl should be taking the lead—I thought perhaps it was some game she'd suggested. And Miss Ambrose sort of fell in with it, like you might humor a kid, though she hadn't been keen at the start. But no, I wouldn't say they were furtive."

As the woman spoke, an unpleasantly grotesque image formed in Clare's mind—of Primrose decoying Ianthe Ambrose away and pushing her into the swimming pool. She wondered if the same fantasy had occurred to Nigel. Oddly enough, it had.

Nigel took this eyewitness's name and cabin number. Then he spoke again to the audience in general.

"No one else any contribution? Right. Now this is going to be tiresome for you; but I want all of you to go away and write down your movements yesterday—where you were, and who was with you, from 9 P.M. till 10:30: make as detailed and accurate a timetable of your movements as possible, please. The police in Athens are bound to question all of us on this point, so we might as well have the answers ready for them. It would be helpful, too," continued Nigel, with no change of tone or expression, "to know where everyone was from midday, say, while the ship was lying at Kalymnos."

"I'm afraid I cannot see the point of that," remarked Jeremy Street, rather loudly. "Miss Ambrose was not murdered on—"

"There may be no point in it. On the other hand, if we all think back hard over yesterday, something may be turned up which will provide a clue to the murderer. And of course, it goes without saying, if any of you had seen or heard anything during the cruise which you now feel may have some bearing on these crimes, come and tell me about it; first-hand evidence only, not hearsay. I shall be in the first officer's cabin, on the bridge deck, from ten o'clock."

Mrs. Hale muttered to Clare, "Is it permitted to ask the lecturer questions?"

Clare grinned. "Try, and see."

Mrs. Hale rose to her feet. "If we know about people who had motives for one of these crimes, do we tell you, or would that be considered idle gossip?"

The audience froze into a deep silence.

"By all means tell me. In private." Nigel paused, eying the passengers meditatively. "There are several people on board who had strongish motives for killing Miss Ambrose. But this does not make them murderers. I must also tell you that there is a suspected professional blackmailer on board. Anyone who has suffered from this person's attentions would be well advised to inform me."

Nigel bowed briefly to the Captain, who raised his hand in a half salute, then strode out of the saloon, his departure starting a buzz of conversation.

V

Clare caught up with him, and led him to a quiet spot on the boat deck.

"That woman's evidence was curious, wasn't it?" she said.

"Yes."

"Considering the way Ianthe flew out at Primrose yesterday morning, when we were queuing up at the gang-way—"

"Yes?"

"One wonders what the child said to her last night, that made Ianthe go with her to—to wherever they went."

"One does."

Nigel appeared extremely distrait; but Clare could never be sure that, behind even his glassiest-eyed look, his brain was not taking in what she said. So she went on:

"I got a fantastic picture in my mind's eye just now. I saw Primrose pushing Ianthe into the swimming pool."

"Yes," said Nigel, staring at the waves bustling and jostling past the ship's white side. "So did I."

"Absurd, wasn't it?"

Nigel turned slowly and faced her, his back to the rail. "Why would you push someone into a swimming pool?"

"Because I was in a rage with her, perhaps," Clare answered. "Primrose gave Ianthe a pretty lethal look yesterday morning."

"Or?"

"Well, let me think. To see if she could swim?"

Nigel's pale eyes blazed. "Now there, my love, you *have* something."

"But we know Ianthe couldn't swim."

"All we know is that she *didn't* swim. The Bishop told me that, when she was a girl, she went through an athletic phase—trying to be a boy, to win her father's love. It'd be surprising if she didn't learn then."

"You can find out easily enough. Ask Faith Trubody. But I don't see what—"

"It'd explain the two splashes I heard. Primrose pushes Ianthe in. Ianthe swims a couple of strokes to the side of the bath, seizes Primrose's ankles, drags her in (splash number two), and strangles her, holding her head under the water."

"I should have thought Primrose would run away after pushing her in."

"Not if she wanted to find out whether Ianthe could swim."

"But you wouldn't strangle a child because—do you mean Ianthe suddenly went off her head with rage?"

"That's not the most important question."

"Well, what is?"

"*Why* did Primrose want to know if Ianthe could swim?"

"I see. But of course it's all based on our flimsy notion that—"

"You know, there's something wrong with this case. It's

all too pat, somehow. Neurotic woman, pushed into bath by child, blows her top, drowns child, then in fit of revulsion throws herself overboard."

"I don't see what's so wrong with that."

"Ianthe has been threatening suicide for some time. She goes to the lecture, looking like death. Here's another chance to show up the shortcomings of her *bête noire*, Jeremy Street. Instead, she gives a heavy sigh and slips out after ten minutes of it. What does this suggest—that she can't stand life any more, and is going to end it. But, if she was determined to kill herself then, why on earth should she allow herself to be sidetracked by Primrose? It doesn't make sense."

"Yes. Well, if she was murdered, we know one person at least who couldn't have done it."

"Who?"

"The *bête noire*. He was lecturing away till about nine-thirty, wasn't he?"

"To be sure." . . .

Peter and Faith were sitting on the sun deck below the bridge, their backs against the bulwark. As Nigel approached, he got the impression of two young animals huddled together for warmth or comfort. Peter scrambled politely to his feet, but gave Nigel a look both defiant and wary.

"Got the handcuffs ready?" he muttered.

"Why do you say that?"

"I was heard threatening Miss Ambrose. Miss Ambrose disappears. Q.E.D."

"Don't be an ass, Peter," said Faith nervously.

"*Did* you murder Miss Ambrose?" asked Nigel.

"Well, really!" Peter Trubody was once again the prefect, speaking in the shocked, superior tone of one who censures a breach of public-school etiquette.

"If you didn't, keep out of my hair. Miss Trubody, did Ianthe ever use the swimming bath at school?"

Faith's lips fell open, showing the pointed incisors.

"What an extraordinary—! No, she didn't, as far as I know. Why?"

"Think hard. You never had any reason to imagine she could swim?"

"Why, no. Actually, she never took part in any of our games. Despised them, I suppose. She used to go on about the system trying to turn us into substitute boys. I don't know why she was so bitter about it. Sour grapes, I expect. Imagine the Bross trying to wield a hockey stick!"

So that is it, thought Nigel. Ianthe, as a child, dismally failed to win her father's heart by making herself good at sport, by becoming a "substitute boy." So then she reacted violently against games. But she could still have learned to swim in those distant days. So we're back where we started. . . . Only, *why* should she have said to me, "I can't swim"? Why not, "I don't like swimming"? Another tiny, nagging, probably irrelevant question.

Nigel's reverie was broken Faith, who whispered to her twin brother, "Why don't you tell him?"

"What's the point? It was obviously my mistake. After all, she went to the lecture—I saw her going up on to the boat deck."

"But it was a very peculiar thing for Mrs. Blaydon to do."

"Don't be so potty, Faith. It only looked peculiar *then*. I was a long way off, remember. And I didn't know then that she'd got sunstroke: that explains everything."

"Well, I still think—"

Brother and sister were arguing in undertones, apparently oblivious of Nigel, who sensed that this argument had taken place before, with no agreement reached.

"My hearing is preternaturally acute," he remarked, smiling. "What *is* all this about?"

Faith began to say, "I keep telling Peter that, in a criminal investigation, any fact may prove useful."

"Too true."

"And when it's something so peculiar—"

"Faith, I absolutely forbid you to—"

"Oh, don't be so stuffy and pompous!" exclaimed the girl, without acrimony.

"*I'll* tell *you* something about criminal investigations," Peter continued. "The police are always having their time wasted by nitwits and busybodies who trot out absurd theories and irrelevant facts."

"That also is true," said Nigel. "But only the chap in charge of the investigation can decide what's relevant."

"What happened yesterday afternoon can't possibly affect the case," said Peter dogmatically. Then he flushed, looking suddenly much younger. "Besides, it's not my secret alone. There are things a gentleman doesn't talk about."

"Oh poof!" exclaimed Faith, giggling. "You told *me.*"

"You're different. You're my tiresome, titivating, tumbledown twin."

The two began to roll about on the deck like puppies, tickling each other. Nigel left them to it, but made a mental note that Peter must be questioned later. For the present, there was the interview with the bereaved Mr. Chalmers, which Nigel frankly dreaded.

VI

The discipline of his profession made Primrose's father a good witness. At any rate, he kept his emotions distinct from his reason and seemed to have himself well under control. Unfortunately, so far as the events of the previous night were concerned, he had nothing to contribute. He had been a little surprised that Primrose should leave the lecture, for she was interested in Jeremy Street's subject; but her parents had never subjected the child to unnatural regulations. It was understood that she would put herself to bed when she felt sleepy; however, when she did not rejoin them after the lecture, and was not to be found in the cabin, her mother had become a little anxious and they had looked for her along the decks, in the saloons and the reading room.

Nigel studied the man sitting opposite him in the first officer's cabin. A smallish man, with a smooth face and a brow that curved back baldly a long way toward the top of his head: the eyes had that mild, attentive yet somehow unfocused look which Nigel had noted before—the look of a man listening; listening, as the analyst must, for implications, overtones, buried voices, both in his patients and in himself.

"At dinner, how did she strike you?" asked Nigel, groping as it were for a light switch in the bewildering, disorientating darkness of this case. "Did she give any signs of apprehension, say, or excitement?"

"I would say she had a secret," Mr. Chalmers brought out after a pause. "She had been thinking out something for herself; or making a plan. Yes, that would be my interpretation."

"You say '*had been*' thinking something out. For some time?"

Mr. Chalmers smoothed his massive brow. "I observed that Primrose was unusually silent yesterday afternoon, after we had bathed."

"Could you tell me about this—all the detail you remember?"

In his practiced way, Mr. Chalmers marshaled the facts. "We visited the Venetian castro, picnicked on a hill nearby, then rested for a while. My wife wanted to bathe, but did not know just where the bathing beaches were situated. So we walked down to the port, and then at a venture took a track leading westward out of the town, above the sea. Presently we came to a cove—about a mile from the port, I think. Miss Ambrose and her sister were sunbathing among the rocks on the far side. It looked a good place for a bathe, but they told us it was infested with sea urchins. So we went on further."

"Which of them told you this?"

"Miss Ambrose. I thought it might be an irrational phobia of hers, but my wife did not like Primrose to risk the sea-urchin possibility."

"Did Mrs. Blaydon say anything?"

"I do not think so. She waved when we left them. Her sister said there was a better beach further on."

"What time was this meeting?"

"I am always very vague about time." Mr. Chalmers' thin lips stretched in a simulacrum of a smile. "It would be, perhaps, around three o'clock."

"And then?"

"We moved on, about half a mile, till we found another beach. We bathed. Then Primrose wandered off by herself."

"Which way did she go?"

"Back along the track we'd come by."

"How long was she absent?"

"I have little idea. My wife and I were discussing a theory of Melanie Klein's in relation to one of my patients."

"Five minutes? An hour?"

"Perhaps half an hour. Not, I think, less. It was when Primrose returned that I got the impression of the feeling tone I mentioned."

"What gave it to you?"

"Primrose seemed distrait, absorbed in some—how shall I describe it?—some problem or speculation of her own. She sat down apart from me, which was of course symptomatic."

"Just sat and thought?"

"She took out her notebook and began to write. But her pen had run dry, so she borrowed a pencil from me."

Nigel held his breath for a few seconds, then asked, "An indelible pencil?"

"No, an ordinary one." A barely perceptible wrinkling on Mr. Chalmers' huge brow was the only indication that he had felt anything odd in Nigel's last question.

"You did not, then or later, ask your daughter what was on her mind?"

"Certainly not." Mr. Chalmers' tone was mildly repressive. "The privacy of the child must always be respected."

"She was under analysis herself, she told me."

"Yes. With a colleague of mine."

The ship's telegraph clanged. Nigel passed his cigarette packet to Mr. Chalmers and lit up.

"You are being most helpful. Will you carry on from there?"

"About half an hour later, we started back toward the harbor. We had a few words with Mrs. Blaydon. She told us she'd bathed after all."

"Where did you meet her?"

"On the far side of the cove—the eastern side; she'd moved over, I suppose, to keep in the sun. Her bathing things and dress were spread out to dry on the rocks. She had on a bathrobe."

"In the sun?"

"Yes. On the western side there's a sharp drop from the track to the rocks, with a shoulder of hill rising just above the track. All that side was in shadow."

"And her sister—had she bathed?"

"I couldn't say. Mrs. Blaydon told us that Miss Ambrose had gone on ahead; she said we might catch up with her."

"Did you?"

"No. She must have gone out to the ship before we reached the quay."

"Mrs. Blaydon gave no reason why her sister had gone on ahead?"

"No. I remember thinking it was almost the first time I'd noticed them apart. Miss Ambrose was something of an emotional vampire I should say."

"Can you give a rough timing for this?"

"No. Wait a minute. Yes, I can. I looked at my watch and told Mrs. Blaydon the *Menelaos* would be leaving in three-quarters of an hour's time. So it must have been 5:15."

Nigel leaned back in his chair. His questions had been following the only line that seemed open to him; but, although it had disclosed one or two curious facts, and one really promising detail, Nigel did not see how this line could lead him toward the murderer.

"During the afternoon, did you see any other passengers, apart from Mrs. Blaydon and Miss Ambrose?"

"Not after we walked out of the town. I'd noticed Mr. Street and that Bentinck-Jones fellow on the quayside then."

"Nothing at all that struck you as peculiar?"

"Well, I did notice, when we got back to the quay, that young Trubody seemed in a bad way."

"What? Ill, you mean?"

"I judged he had had a severe shock, or was in some acute emotional crisis. He rejected my overtures very abruptly. Wasn't talking to anyone. He didn't come out on the caique with us—caught a later one, I presume."

"Yes," said Nigel, "he only just made it. He and Mrs. Blaydon."

VII

Mr. Chalmers had only just left the cabin when there was a knock on the door, and Faith Trubody came in, followed by Jeremy Street. Nigel got the impression that the lecturer had been towed in, rather against his better judgment; at any rate, he stood negligently aside, as if dissociating himself from the proceedings, looking around at the appointments of the first officer's cabin. His lined, handsome face seemed more of a façade than ever—a façade which might at any moment crumble—revealing what? The real man, or emptiness?

"Jeremy's being blackmailed," the girl breathlessly exclaimed. "I told him he must tell you about it. Of course, it may not have anything to do with the murder, but a man who could do that could—"

"Just a minute," Nigel put in. "Could you start at the beginning. And do sit down, won't you, Miss Trubody."

Faith plumped herself down on the first officer's bed.

"It's that horrible little man, Bentinck-Jones. He was spying on us on the hillside. Jeremy saw something flashing and then—"

"My dear girl," protested Jeremy, a cold irritation in his voice, "if we must wash dirty linen in public—"

"Dirty linen!" A slightly malicious look appeared on the girl's face. "When you asked me to marry you!"

Jeremy Street gave her a furiously angry glance; then, controlling himself, speaking in a clipped voice, told the story. When he had finished, Nigel said:

"But I don't understand what's worrying you. You say that Bentinck-Jones saw you and Miss Trubody in what he interpreted as a compromising situation. He followed you down to the quayside, after you had left her, and threatened to tell her father what he had seen. Right?"

"Yes."

"But what proof could he have, to convince Mr. Trubody? It'd be your word, and Faith's, against his, wouldn't it?"

Jeremy Street's head, with its bleached golden hair, shied away like a horse's. "He had a camera, with a telephoto lens," he said, his lips barely moving.

"I see. Has he shown you a print?"

"Not yet."

"I don't know why you didn't bash up his camera, or throw it into the sea," cried Faith.

"Oh, really! This isn't an American movie."

"You see, Jeremy is trying to interest Daddy in some project; and if—"

"For God's sake, keep out of this, Faith!" Jeremy turned to Nigel. "What we—I—wondered was if you couldn't put pressure on Bentinck-Jones and get the film out of his hands."

"Pressure? What pressure?" said Nigel unsympathetically. "I'm supposed to be conducting a murder investigation."

"That's the whole point," said Faith, her green eyes gazing full at Nigel. "You see, last night—just before 9:15 it was

—I saw this foul little Bentinck-Jones come up the staircase from where Miss Ambrose's cabin is, and go out on the deck toward the swimming pool."

"You're accusing him of the murder?"

"Well, it's jolly suspicious, isn't it?"

"And the idea is that I should use this information to get back the film from him? Did anyone else see him go out toward the fo'c's'le then?"

"I haven't a clue. I was alone."

"But why don't you do it yourself? If it's a question of blackmailing the blackmailer—"

"This is getting us nowhere," interrupted Jeremy, with a supercilious air. "I should have thought that, as you are in charge of the investigation, you could have the fellow's cabin searched."

"It was searched last night," said Nigel.

"Indeed? Then—"

"But not for camera film."

"Well, then," said the girl, "search it again."

Jeremy threw up his hands in a theatrical gesture of despair.

"While we're about it," Nigel said, "have you two written out your movements last night?"

Jeremy Street took a sheet of paper from his pocket and handed it to Nigel, who glanced at it.

9–9:30 *lecturing on boat deck.*
9:30–9:35 *(approx.) talked with a few members of audience.*
9:35 *went to own cabin.*
9:40 *went to bar on afterdeck.*
10:00 *showed up at dance.*

"Have you corroboration of all this?" Nigel asked.

"I was in full view of about fifty people while I lectured. I don't know the names of the people I talked to after it, though I could pick them out if you held an identification parade. I've no idea if anyone saw me go to my cabin—the man who shares it with me was not there. The bartender may or may not remember my drinking from nine-forty to ten; there was a crowd of Frogs at the bar. Faith will confirm that I turned up at the dance about ten, and stayed there."

Ignoring the man's deliberately riling tone, Nigel turned to Faith.

"Do you confirm it?"

"Oh, I expect so. I wasn't watching the clock, though."

"And what about your movements?"

"I was in the saloon, waiting for the dance to begin, from about nine o'clock. Peter and my father were with me."

"Did you leave the saloon at any time between nine and ten?"

"Oh no."

"Then how did you see Mr. Bentinck-Jones creeping out on deck to murder Primrose?"

Faith bit her thin lower lip, flushing. "I suppose you think that's very clever. I happened to be standing by the glass door into the saloon. That's how I saw him come up the stairs. He went out on deck, and turned right, toward the bow of the ship."

"Right," said Nigel briskly, "thank you. I shall not need you any more, Miss Trubody."

The girl hesitated, gave Jeremy a dipping, sliding look, then made her exit.

"Faith seems to be a congenital liar," Jeremy offered. "Like most women."

Nigel made no direct comment on this. "Going back to yesterday afternoon," he said, "did you in fact ask her to marry you, or is that another of her fictions?"

"I did. She refused."

"How very odd."

A ghost of a smile on Jeremy's face revealed that he took Nigel's remark as a compliment to his eligibility. "She's a bit of a delinquent, if you ask me—told me she wanted sexual experience, not marriage."

This unusual, if unlikable, forthcomingness suggested to Nigel that the man was feeling relief because they had moved away from dangerous ground, or was babbling to divert the talk from it. He cast about with random questions, on this side and that, waiting for the signs—an involuntary gesture, a too guarded look, or a feel of greater tension in the air—which told his instinct, trained by much questioning of suspects, that the probe was nearing a sensitive spot.

"Bentinck-Jones wanted money, I take it?"

"Presumably. His approach was exceedingly devious, though."

"Did you promise him any?"

"Gracious, no. I stalled."

"Where did this happen?"

"On the quay. I shook him off presently, and took a boat back to the ship. I wanted to get—to think things out."

The asdic in Nigel's mind faintly pinged. Jeremy Street had altered the course of his last sentence; what had he "wanted to get"?

"But you came ashore again. You returned later in the same caique as Miss Massinger and myself."

"That is so."

"Where did you go, the second time?"

"A little way out of the port. Westward. I found a bit of shade and read a book."

The asdic had gone silent again.

"What book?" asked Nigel, quite at a loss for his next move. The effect of this imbecile question was, however, astonishing. Jeremy Street's handsome head tossed up; he smoothed the hair at the back of it with trembling fingers; his finely chiseled mouth looked suddenly botched. "What a damned, silly, impertinent question!" he exclaimed.

"Silly, I expect. But why impertinent?"

"I use the word in the sense of not pertinent, irrelevant."

"You don't remember the name of the book?"

"Now look here! I—" Jeremy visibly took a grip on himself. With an ingratiating smile, he went on, "No, actually I don't. It was some thriller I took out of the ship's library. Fact is, I didn't read much—couldn't get that swine Bentinck-Jones off my mind."

After a slight pause, Nigel asked, "From where you were sitting, could you see that track which leads westward out of the town?"

"Yes. I was above it, on the hillside."

"See anyone you knew passing along?"

"I saw Primrose Chalmers and her parents, walking back toward the town."

"Any idea of the time?"

"Yes. I looked at my watch to see if it was time for me to start back. It was between 5:20 and 5:25."

"Miss Ambrose must have walked along the track before then. You didn't notice her."

"No."

Nigel seemed to sense a return of the tension, which had eased after they left the subject of Street's reading matter.

"Nothing else you saw, or heard?"

"I don't think so. Oh, there was someone—but it could have been a goat scrambling about on the hillside above me. Earlier. Perhaps an hour before the Chalmerses passed by."

A goat, perhaps, thought Nigel; or perhaps a human goat —one that knew the island well.

VIII

Nigel felt he could get little further till he had interviewed Melissa Blaydon. A sea breeze blew in at the cabin window, fluttering its curtain and tempering the heat of the day. Looking out, he saw sea and sky, and an island hazily remote.

He sat down again, and began to write on a sheet of foolscap paper. It was his custom, in the lull of an investigation, to compile an anthology of oddities—scraps of information, dialogue, query, observation, which had struck him as anomalous and therefore challenging, set down haphazard as they came to mind. Three more cigarette stubs were piled in the ashtray before he had finished.

1. Ianthe. Sunstroke, but returned ship alone.
2. "Bathing things and dress spread out to dry on the rocks." Slip of tongue? Freudian? If not, why?
3. A lot of wetness about—Nikki's evidence.
4. What was Jeremy reading? Pornography?—not just after episode with Faith. What would he be humiliated by being known to have read? Or did he return ship to get, not a book, but ? ? ?
5. Faith needs her bottom spanked. Would take Ianthe's word against hers over trouble at school?
6. What did Peter see on Kalymnos? "I didn't know then that she'd got sunstroke." See (1). Sunstroke explained some peculiar action of Melissa's—something that gave P. "severe shock," acute emotional crisis. ? ? ? Well, go and ask him, you silly coot.
7. Pencil, not fountain pen. First importance—follow up. Pressure. Film.
8. Primrose's "secret," her "plan"—to do with Ianthe? Surely. Why do you push someone into swimming pool? Clare hit jackpot ? ?
9. Nikki said C. and I, mistaken about seeing him walk away from harbor. A lie. Yet he came clean about episode in Melissa's cabin. Highly significant?
10. Why did M. struggle in silence? Why struggle at all?—she'd made assignation with Nikki. No, we've only his word for this. Ask her.
11. No bathing cap in shower? Looks bad. See (3).
12. Can Bentinck-Jones's movements be checked? Under what circumstances could the victim, not the blackmailer, be murdered?

Nigel brooded over this odd assortment, pushing the pieces about, trying to fit them into one another. Several of them he fairly soon discarded, as if, coming from some different puzzle, they had got into the wrong box. But the remainder—it was astonishing, the way they built up into a section of a picture, of a fantastic picture which, Nigel now realized, he had already, without knowing it, half glimpsed from time to time.

He added two more entries on the foolscap sheet:

13. Landing tickets. Awkward, but could be fiddled; especially by Nikki.
14. Clare: the Bishop: Melissa at Delos. Swans.

As Nigel folded the sheet and pocketed it, the cruise manager entered with a sheaf of papers.

"They are nearly complete. I've put them in alphabetical order."

"Very kind. Did anyone refuse to give us a statement?"

"No, *sir*. I didn't trouble Mrs. Blaydon or the Chalmerses, of course. And Miss Trubody told me she gave you the data orally."

"You've included an account of your *own* movements last night?"

Nikki looked wounded. "Sure, sure. Why wouldn't I? Oh, and there's a radio message from Scotland Yard just come in."

Nigel read it. Ivor Bentinck-Jones was known to Records as a confidence trickster. Did a stretch in 1947. No conviction since.

"Changed his profession," remarked Nigel. "What *were* you doing on Kalymnos, my friend?"

Nikki's lustrous eyes filmed over. "Say, what's biting you, Mr. Strangeways?"

"Well, the Athenian police can find out—and I don't suppose their methods are as polite as mine."

"Kalymnos, as your great dramatist Gilbert Sullivan wrote, is nothing to do with the case."

"Then why bother to lie about your movements there?"

"Sir! You insult me!" Nikki quivered to the eyelashes with outrage. "We Greeks are a proud people—"

"Are you, personally, too proud to burgle Mr. Bentinck-Jones's cabin?"

"That rat!" The mercurial Nikki beamed. "I will beat him up for you. Anything."

"After I've had a word with Mrs. Blaydon, ask Bentinck-Jones to come along here. Then you can search his cabin. You're looking for camera film this time. I doubt if we have authority for this, but it can't be helped. Don't go breaking things open, though, or you may get into trouble. Just collect any film or photographs you find lying about. Oh, and one thing more—" Nigel gave Nikki a steady look—"is it possible to get in touch with Kalymnos by radio-telephone?"

"Sure."

"Then will you ask the Captain to do so. I want the authorities on Kalymnos to search around that bathing place you recommended to Mrs. Blaydon."

"Search the—? But, Mr. Strangeways, whatever for?" The look of bewilderment, or consternation, on the cruise manager's face was almost comical.

"They should search the little bay, and the land between it and the harbor, on either side of the track. They will be looking for clues, Nikki, clues—something a murderer left behind him," said Nigel with urgency, his eyes fixed on the other man, who was staring at him as if Nigel had diabolical powers. "Will you first go and find the Bishop of Solway. Ask him if he will step up here, please."

Nikki departed, scratching his bristly blue jowl. Nigel picked out of the sheaf of papers the statements written by Peter Trubody, Ivor Bentinck-Jones, and Nikki himself. These, with Jeremy Street and Faith Trubody, who had already given him the information, were the only people on board whom Nigel knew or suspected had motives for murdering Ianthe Ambrose.

Peter's statement said that he had been sitting with his family in the forward lounge from about 8:45 the previous evening. He had remained there till the dance started, except for a minute or two—he could not give the exact time—when his sister had asked him to fetch a stole from her cabin. Thereafter, he was dancing, or talking with Mrs. Blaydon at the bar, till ten-thirty.

Ivor Bentinck-Jones—his handwriting had a crabbed, secretive look compared with Peter Trubody's careless scrawl—stated that he was in the bar on the afterdeck from the end of dinner till about 9:15. He then went below to get a clean handkerchief, having used the one in his pocket to mop his trouser leg, on which he had spilled some drink. "I then observed the cruise manager entering Mrs. Blaydon's cabin, under the circumstances of which I have already apprised you and am prepared to testify on my oath." After this episode Bentinck-Jones had gone up on deck for a breath of air before the dance began. He was in the forward lounge from then on.

Nikki's statement was a good deal more elaborate, and not so precise. He had gone up to the boat deck at about ten to nine, to see that all was in readiness for the lecture. His duties had then taken him to various other parts of the ship. At 9:15 he went to Mrs. Blaydon's cabin, was repulsed, retired to brush his hair and lick his wounds, appeared in the forward lounge between 9:25 and 9:30.

The three statements seemed unexceptionable. One would have to make sure that Faith had asked Peter to fetch her stole. Bentinck-Jones's information about spilling the drink struck Nigel as a bit overzealous; but the man could not have premeditated the murder of Primrose Chalmers at this period, for he could not have known that she would slip out of the lecture early.

The Nikki-Melissa episode still seemed peculiar. Knowing that the lecture would be over at 9:30, was it not odd that she should make an assignation with Nikki for 9:15? Only a quarter of an hour before her sister might be expected to return? Whatever one might think of Melissa, she was surely not the quick-time tart. Was it possible that she had never, in fact, made the assignation, that Nikki had seen her enter her cabin and decided to try his luck? He had had encouragement enough, in all conscience.

The subject of Nigel's thoughts now ushered in the Bishop of Solway.

"No, don't go, Nikki." Nigel turned to the Bishop. "Would you help me, sir? Nikki's going to get through to

Kalymnos on the radio-telephone. Will you be present when he does so?"

The Bishop looked no less puzzled by his request than Nikki.

"You understand Greek," said Nigel. "I just want to be sure that the message isn't—er—garbled."

"Well, bless my soul!" The Bishop shot a keen glance at Nikki, who stood there with his mouth open like an operatic tenor about to launch upon some great, protesting aria. "Very well. What is the message?"

Nigel told him.

IX

It was now barely eleven-thirty. But no passengers had come to volunteer evidence, and Nigel was eager to get the next interview over with; he rather dreaded it, but so much depended upon it. Running Dr. Plunket to earth in his surgery, he asked if it would be possible to talk with Mrs. Blaydon now.

"Well, I said midday, but I don't suppose half an hour will make any difference. I'm afraid I must insist on being present, though. She's my patient, and she's been badly knocked up."

"By all means, be present, I'll make it as short and easy for her as I can."

The doctor entered Melissa's cabin first. Then, putting his head out, he beckoned Nigel in.

The cabin was stuffy with heat and a stale smell of eau-de-cologne, though an electric fan was working at full pressure. The linen curtains were drawn over the porthole, muting the light to a kind of dusk. It was one of the most expensive cabins on the *Menelaos,* with twin beds instead of tiered bunks. On one of these lay the bereaved woman, propped up with pillows, one languid brown arm lying on the white counterpane, the other hand supporting her beautiful head, which was half veiled with a yellow silk handkerchief. Even in the shock of grief, Nigel observed her instinct for the attractive pose had not deserted her. She was, as always, exquisitely made up; but her features seemed a little coarsened by the ordeal she had been undergoing.

"It's awfully good of you to see me," said Nigel. "Please accept my sympathy. It's been a horrible shock for you, and I'll try to badger you as little as possible. At least it may save you hours of questioning by the police when we get to Athens."

"Do sit down, Mr. Strangeways—Nigel, if I may call you that." With a faint gesture of the hand that lay on the counterpane, she indicated the twin bed. "This dear man —" her eyes glanced toward Dr. Plunket—"has told me you are a famous detective. I'd never have thought it. Now, what do you wish to ask me?"

Grief had given the woman a dignity, a calm, which she had not shown before in their brief acquaintance, thought Nigel; the gamine element was no longer in evidence.

"When did you last see your sister?"

"After dinner last night. I brought her some grapes."

"What was her state of mind then?"

"Well, she was very silent. But she did say her headache was much better, and that she'd be going to the lecture presently. She didn't seem to want me to stay, so I came up to the lounge after sitting with her about ten minutes."

"You got no impression that she was—well, thinking of putting an end to her life?"

"Of course not! I'd never have left her if—I mean, she didn't seem any more depressed than usual. To tell you the truth, I'd begun to doubt if she'd ever been really serious when she talked about suicide."

"Could you just tell me about your own movements, for the record? You came up to the bar?"

"Yes. I had a drink. Then I came down here to dress for the dance."

"What time would that have been?"

"Well, I take rather an age dressing. I allowed myself

forty minutes, the dance was to start at nine-thirty. Yes, so I must have come down about ten to nine."

"And your sister was not here?"

"No. I assumed she'd gone up already, to get a good seat at the lecture."

"I noticed you did not put in an appearance till the second foxtrot had begun. You'd been delayed?"

"Well, I was very hot, so I had a shower. And then a rather tiresome thing happened."

"What was that?"

"Oh, I'd really rather not tell you."

"You don't need to. Nikki has."

The mascaraed lashes fluttered, the head was turned further away from him. "Oh! Oh dear me! But how very extraordinary of him! This is most embarrassing for me. The last thing I want to do is to get the silly man into trouble."

"He says you'd made an—asked him to come and see you at 9:15."

"Does he indeed? Well, I *must* say! I'm afraid the poor doctor is mystified by all this. Doctor, will you *please* let me talk to Mr. Strangeways alone. I promise I won't tire myself."

"Very well. But not more than ten minutes. I'll come back then, Mrs. Blaydon."

She gave Dr. Plunket a grateful, languishing look, and he went out.

"Nikki must have misunderstood something I'd said. I did tell him, in the morning, that perhaps I'd see him before the dance started."

"See him privately?"

"Well, yes. He'd been getting rather troublesome—I mean, I like him, he's very attractive, but I felt the time had come to cool things off a bit. But then he strode in and sort of pounced on me."

"In the dark."

"Yes. It really was a nuisance, you know."

"You were dressing in the dark?"

"I—? Oh, I see. I'd just come from the shower. I suppose he saw me entering the cabin and followed. I was still—I'd just taken off my bathrobe, and was going to turn on the light, when he bounced in."

Nigel pursued it no further. Gazing steadily at the averted head, the exquisite profile standing out from the yellow scarf, he said:

"I'm afraid your sister did not commit suicide."

"*Afraid?* I don't understand. . . . Oh God! She didn't—it's nothing to do with that poor child?"

"We don't know yet. When did you hear about Primrose?"

"Last night. After the dance. A rumor went around—they'd been appealing on the loud-speaker. Then one of the officers told us. It's the most horrible thing. I'd been down here to look for Ianthe; she wasn't in the cabin—it was about eleven o'clock then, and she didn't usually stay up late. I looked for her on the decks everywhere—that was when the officer told me about Primrose—but I couldn't find her. So I asked Nikki to broadcast a message for her on the loud-speaker."

"Melissa, you must prepare yourself for a worse—"

"I know what you're going to tell me." She was staring straight in front of her. "Ianthe was murdered. Isn't that it?"

Nigel did not need to reply.

"Have they found her—her body?"

"No."

"I don't know what to say"—her voice was nearly a wail—"I just don't know what to say. I was afraid of this."

"Afraid she'd be—? Have you any suspicions about who might have done it?"

"Well, she did get her knife into people, poor Ianthe. Mr. Street, for instance."

There was silence. Then Nigel said, carefully picking his words, "I won't bother you with the reasons, but I believe the clue to the murders is on Kalymnos."

"On Kalymnos?" It came out in a ghostly echo.

"Yes. It'd be the greatest help to me if you described exactly what you and your sister did after you went ashore yesterday."

For the first time she looked at Nigel full face; her eyelids were swollen, and there was a bewildered, wild sort of expression in her eyes, as they searched his.

"I'll try. If it's important."

Helped along by an occasional question from Nigel, she told her story. The sisters had explored the little town, bought some postcards, had lunch in the open air outside one of the cafés along the quay, then moved off to find the cove which Nikki had recommended. They met no one on the track which led to it. They must have reached the cove at about two-thirty. They sunbathed for a while—Ianthe had taken to sunbathing the last few days—then Melissa decided to have a swim; the water was deep there, and there were good rocks to dive off. Ianthe, however, spied sea urchins on several of them, below the surface of the water, and urged her sister not to risk bathing off these rocks. It was shortly after this that the Chalmerses had turned up.

"Yes, Mr. Chalmers told me your sister warned them about the sea urchins, and told them there was a safe beach further on. By the way, how did she know there was?"

"Oh, she didn't. She just wanted to get rid of them—particularly the child. Primrose got on her nerves. Well, the fact is, Ianthe was rather possessive in her attitude toward me—you must have noticed it yourself. We hadn't met for so long, and I suppose she liked to have me all to herself."

"So neither of you bathed?"

"Not then. Ianthe never did, anyway."

"She couldn't swim?"

"Well, she didn't swim."

"Never learned, as a child."

"I don't remember. And of course, she might have learned since. But she talked as if she couldn't."

"I see. Will you carry on from there?"

After the Chalmerses' departure, Melissa had gone to sleep. When she woke up, she noticed Ianthe, who was lying beside her, looking ill. She said she had a terrible headache. Melissa tried to move her, away from the sea's edge, into the shade, but Ianthe fainted. Melissa soaked handkerchiefs and put them on her sister's forehead— there was no one in sight, to whom she could call for help. Presently Ianthe began to recover; she was in rather a bad temper, and said she must go back to the ship. Melissa wanted to accompany her, fearing she might not be well enough to get back alone, but Ianthe insisted on going by herself.

"She had some special reason for being alone, did you feel?"

"Special reason?"

"She usually kept at your side so much, I wondered if she'd engaged to meet someone and didn't want you to know about it."

"Oh, I see. Well, now you ask me, she did seem rather impatient to get away. I put it down at the time to her being irritable, after her faint. She didn't really like being so dependent on me."

"It's a sign of convalescence, when people start to get irritable."

The woman glanced at him briefly. "And irritability doesn't fit in with contemplated suicide?"

"Exactly." Melissa's mental processes, thought Nigel, had been sharpened by her loss.

"And you think she might have arranged to meet someone yesterday afternoon, on the island, and that whatever happened between them led to her being murdered last night? That's why you said the clue to the murderer would be found on Kalymnos?"

"It's a theory."

"You think she met her—the person who killed her—on the island?"

"Yes. What time was it when she left you?"

"Oh, goodness, I don't know. I've no idea how long I was asleep."

"Was it half an hour, say, before the time you spoke with the Chalmerses again?"

"About that, perhaps."

"You did bathe, after all, I understand?"

Nigel gathered that, as soon as Ianthe had set off, her sister decided to bathe—Ianthe being no longer there to fuss about sea urchins. When she finally got out, that side of the cove was in shadow, so she moved over to the other side.

"To dry your dress in the sun?"

"Dry my dress?" The lovely face looked momentarily disconcerted.

"Mr. Chalmers told me you had it spread out on a rock to dry."

"Yes. It was maddening. I'd sort of kicked it off a rock by mistake when I was diving in. That's why I nearly missed the ship. I was waiting till it got dry."

"And Peter Trubody was waiting for you?"

"How do you mean?"

"Well, you came back to the ship together."

"Oh, I see. Yes, he was at the quayside. But he wasn't waiting for me, as far as I know."

"He didn't explain why he'd left it so late?"

"No. Actually, I could hardly get a word out of him. He seemed in a very queer state of mind. Oh my God! You don't think?—" Her voice broke off, her slim brown hand clenched on the counterpane.

"What don't I think?"

"That Peter could have—that it was he Ianthe had arranged to meet?"

Whatever Nigel's thoughts were on this subject, he did not enlarge upon them, for Dr. Plunket entered the cabin and firmly told him his time was up.

X

"You can tell Mr. Bentinck-Jones I want to see him now."

Nikki's teeth flashed at Nigel like breakers ahead. "And then I take his cabin to pieces?" he asked with relish.

"You'll probably find the film in his camera."

The camera, however, was slung over its owner's shoulder when he entered, grinning impudently at Nigel.

"And how's the great detective doing? Still baffled?"

Nigel scrutinized him. This man, beneath his professional bonhomie, had neither shame nor compunction; the ordinary weapons, therefore, were useless against him; even the protracted silence with which Nigel greeted his arrival seemed to cause him no uneasiness whatsoever. He sat down on the bed and lit a cigarette.

"What are your commands, dear sir?" said Ivor at last.

"I hear you've been at it again."

"At it? That depends on what you mean," Ivor blithely remarked.

"Not what you got a stretch for ten years ago."

"Well, well, so we've been digging up the past, have we?"

"We have. And the present. I'll come to that in a minute. Who do you think committed these murders?"

"I haven't your facilities for collecting evidence. Why ask me?"

"Because your profession demands a close study of people's weaknesses."

"My profession?"

"Or hobby, or whatever you call it."

"I'm afraid you have the advantage of me."

"You're damn right I have. Mr. Street has told me all about your conversation with him."

The man's pudgy, impudent face took on a guarded look. He puffed a little faster at his cigarette, before replying.

"Mr. Street is an imaginative man. What was his version of this alleged conversation?"

Nigel told him—spinning it out, for Nikki must be given time, but not mentioning the photograph with which Bentinck-Jones had threatened Street. "Are you denying that you tried to extort money from him by threats?"

"Of course I deny it. You have no proof at all of his story."

"You admit nothing?"

"I admit I saw him and Miss Trubody in a compromising position." The man's tongue licked at the side of his mouth, as if to retrieve a crumb of some dainty he had been eating.

"So you're just a harmless old voyeur?"

"I disapprove of elderly men corrupting minors. It is the public duty of any citizen to expose that sort of thing. Or don't you agree?" Ivor made no attempt to conceal the cynicism of his utterance.

"How nice for you, to get moral satisfaction as well as a cash payment out of your hobby. Would you say Jeremy Street was capable of strangling minors as well as corrupting them?"

"There was no question of cash payment," the man replied rather perfunctorily. "Street is an egotist, of course, and conceited. Such people do not tolerate obstacles, in my experience."

"Your prison experience? You met some homicides there?"

Ivor grinned like a dog. "I thought our chat was taking a friendlier tone. My mistake."

"Has it occurred to you that, if Street is a desperate character who won't tolerate obstacles, he's a dangerous one to blackmail?"

"I've no doubt he would be," Ivor equably replied. "But, as I've told you, I did not blackmail him."

"What is your version of the talk you had with him yesterday afternoon?"

Bentinck-Jones related it, in a leisurely way. The gist of it was that he had told Street what he had seen, and that he would feel it his duty to inform Faith Trubody's father, unless Street undertook to lay off the girl.

Shortly after this, Nikki appeared at the cabin door, looking crestfallen. He shook his head at Nigel, who at once said, "I think this gentleman has some film he would like developed. Is there someone on the ship who can do it for him?"

"Sure, sure."

"Your camera, please." Nigel stretched his hand toward Bentinck-Jones, who rose to his feet, exclaiming:

"What the hell is all this? I absolutely refuse—"

"Take it from him, Nikki."

Nikki placed his hand on Ivor's head, pushed down hard so that he folded on the bed like a concertina, and whipped the camera off him. There was a roll of film inside it.

"I forgot to tell you," said Nigel, when Nikki had left, "that Jeremy Street mentioned you'd been taking photographs."

Bentinck-Jones gave him one poisoned-dart look. "I shall complain to the Captain, the owners! This is outrageous!"

"I know. Robbery on the high seas. Talking of which, what did Primrose Chalmers write at the end of that notebook you pinched off her body?"

Ivor's eyes swiveled about the cabin. He puffed himself out, but the tone of outrage was wearing thin. "I don't know what you mean."

"The rest of her notebook was written in ink, which ran and became indecipherable through exposure to sea water in the swimming pool. But Mr. Chalmers tells me that her last entry was made in pencil. You could read this. You did read it, before throwing the notebook overboard. What did she say?"

"I never touched any bloody notebook!" The man's voice had taken on a jailbird's whine.

"That's unlucky for you. If you'd been able to give me this information, it might have made things easier for you. As it is, with that photograph you took . . ."

Nigel was bluffing all around. The negative might not be in the camera; perhaps it did not even exist—Bentinck-Jones himself could have been bluffing when he told Street he had photographed him and Faith.

"What is your proposition?" asked Ivor.

"Under certain circumstances, Jeremy Street might be persuaded to keep his mouth shut."

"Don't make me laugh! Of course he will. He can't afford to have a scandal—not where Mr. Trubody is concerned."

"Hadn't you thought," asked Nigel affably, "of blackmailing Trubody himself? All that dough. And his daughter's reputation."

Bentinck-Jones shrugged his shoulders. "I asked you what's your proposition?"

"Very well, you lay off Street and I'll lay off you; but I must know what was in Primrose's notebook."

"That's a most immoral idea—compounding a felony, eh?" The fat little man chuckled. "And if I won't play?"

"I hand you over to the Greek police and pass on my information about you to Scotland Yard, whether Street agrees or not."

"Nothing doing," said Ivor with a sneer.

"I thought not. You're forgetting this is a murder investigation. I have a witness who saw you going out on deck behind Primrose, just before she was murdered."

"You're bluffing."

"I'll ask her to repeat her statement to your face." Nigel moved toward the door.

"Wait a minute, wait a minute! I swear I had nothing to do with the child's death."

"And then, after her body had been discovered, you were seen taking an unhealthy interest in it. You stole her notebook because you were afraid it contained damning evidence about your blackmailing activities."

"This is absolutely preposterous!"

"The police in Athens won't take that view. Good morning."

Bentinck-Jones was rattled at last. "If I tell you what she

wrote—but it doesn't *mean* anything," he almost wailed.

"That's for me to judge."

"You'll guarantee the—the other matter will go no further?"

"I'm giving no guarantees," said Nigel harshly. "I'm interested in the case against you as a murderer, not a blackmailer. If you are innocent, you'd better co-operate. If you don't co-operate, the police will take you to pieces. They can be quite rough, you know."

Bentinck-Jones's effrontery was all gone. Nigel had found his weak spot at last: the man was a physical coward. This accounted for the devious, insinuating approach he made to his prospective victims.

"It doesn't make sense—what she wrote," Ivor was muttering. "I can't remember the exact words, but it was something like this: 'A. is a liar. She said she couldn't swim, but she can—at least, I'm almost certain she can. Because B. always wore a yellow bathing cap, and the one I saw didn't. I couldn't see properly, I was too far away and there were rocks in between. But she swam out to fetch the wicker case, which was floating away. I thought it was a seal at first, but of course there aren't seals in Greece. I saw the case, and then the arm reaching for it out of the sea, and the black head. Then she disappeared back under the rocks. Why did she never bathe when other people were there? Perhaps she has a deformity.' Am I going too fast?"

Nigel was taking it down on a sheet of paper.

"No. Carry on."

"There was a bit about how she hated A. and would love to show her up. The whole thing was childish. Then she'd written: 'I suppose it *could* have been B., or some third person, even—but there were only the two when we went by. How can I prove it? A. is a foul bitchy hypocrite. She insulted me. I shall make a plan and bide my time and have my revenge.'"

Bentinck-Jones smiled tentatively. "Quite a vindictive infant."

"Is that all?"

"The notebook stopped there."

"Are you sure you've remembered everything? Think."

"Yes," said Ivor after a pause. "That's everything she wrote. And much good may it do you," he added with a spurt of viciousness.

"Where were you yesterday, after your conversation with Street?"

"Drinking. On the quayside."

"Till you returned to the ship?"

"Yes."

"Near the jetty?"

"Yes."

"Waiting for Miss Ambrose? What time did she turn up?"

"I don't know what you're talking about."

"You'd made no appointment to meet Miss Ambrose there?"

"Why the hell should I?" said Ivor shakily. "I never set eyes on the woman the whole afternoon."

"What time did you go back to the ship?"

"Oh, about five-thirty, I think."

"You were alone all the time?"

"Yes, but—"

"See any of our friends earlier on?"

"Street came ashore again, by himself, and walked off—which way would it be—out of the town westward."

"Was Nikki about?"

A vindictive look came into Bentinck-Jones's face. "He was. In a manner of speaking."

"What manner of speaking?"

"He pretended not to be. I saw him slinking out of an alley, just beyond that Customs House place or whatever it is. I shouted to him. He edged back out of sight. Later, I asked him what he'd been up to. He denied having been there at all—said I must have been mistaken. You'd do well to keep your eye on him," Ivor concluded, "he's a slippery customer."

"What time was it when you saw this alley-slinking act?"

"Oh, about half an hour before I returned to the ship. Five o'clock, say."

At this point, the subject of their conversation entered and told Nigel there were two passengers outside who urgently wished to speak to him.

"Send them in. That's all, Bentinck-Jones. For the present."

XI

The older of the two women had a sweet, vague, apologetic look. The younger, Nigel surmised, had thrust her into the present interview.

"My aunt has some information for you. Oh, I'm Jane Arthurs, and this is my aunt Emily."

"I'm afraid," said the elder lady, "we are quite unjustifiably trespassing on your time. Shortsightedness, as I keep telling my dear niece, really does rather disqualify me as an eyewitness."

"An eyewitness?" Nikki almost yelped. "You saw the crime, lady?"

"Oh dear no; nothing so—er—helpful as that. I must apologize, Mr. Strangeways, for intruding upon—"

"*Please*, Aunt Emily. Mr. Strangeways *asked* for this information."

"But it *is* so very tenuous," fluttered the older woman, her eyes groping toward Nigel across the few feet that separated them.

After a good deal more of this, Nigel brought her to the point. She had been ascending the staircase that led up from the maindeck cabins to the forward saloon, at about 9:15 last night, when a woman passed her, going down. She thought now that this woman was Miss Ambrose. Yes, it could have been just before 9:15. No, she had only caught a glimpse of the woman out of the corner of her eye, and could not affirm with any conviction that it had been Miss

Ambrose. The woman had run past, in a hurry. She could not vouch for it, but had an impression that the woman was wearing a rug over her head and body.

Emily Arthur's reluctance to come forward was very understandable. As Nikki said, when the two ladies retired, "Where does that get you? The dame's half blind."

"The rug is instructive—or would be, if it was true. Still, I agree, we can't rely on her evidence. Actually, at the moment, I'm less interested in Miss Ambrose's movements than in yours."

"Mine? But I've told you—"

"Your movements yesterday afternoon. Miss Massinger and I saw you creeping off past the Customs House, in a highly furtive and suspicious manner. You denied that it was you we saw. Later, about 5 P.M., Bentinck-Jones saw you creeping back. You told him, too, that he was mistaken. What were you up to?"

Nikki's eyes hardened. He opened his mouth to speak, then shut it again.

"I suggest," pursued Nigel, "that you had an assignation with Mrs. Blaydon at the little cove. You also, to be sure that Melissa would be alone, told Ianthe you wanted a private talk with her at such and such an hour in the afternoon. You didn't intend to keep the later appointment, of course."

Nikki was staring at him, between incredulity and horror.

"On the way to the cove, you unfortunately ran into Miss Ambrose, and what happened then compelled you to kill her."

"Say! This is haywire! Mr. Strangeways, you feeling all right?"

"Mr. Bentinck-Jones said he saw you 'slinking out of an alley.' His choice of words was suggestive. Slinking, alley, alley cat, slinking alley cat, tomcat. What woman had you been with? Mrs. Blaydon, or Miss Ambrose?"

"Neither of them."

"But you'd been with a woman?"

"I'm not talking."

"Maybe the Athens police will lubricate your talking apparatus."

"I am a Greek, a brave man. I am not to be intimidated by thugs." Nikki gave Nigel a look of stern integrity. "If I tell you, you will promise to let it go no further?"

"I'm not making any promises. But if it has no connection with these murders—"

"O.K. then." Nikki beamed, in one of his mercurial changes of mood. "I was laying Aphrodite."

"I *beg* your pardon!"

"She is the most beautiful girl in the Aegean. Oh, boy, what a torso!" Nikki sketched an opulent figure in thin air, and proceeded to an intimate catalogue of the lady's charms.

"But why on earth didn't you tell me this before?"

"Aphrodite's husband is a sponge fisher. He is away from Kalymnos during the summer. He is a strong man— stronger even than I. He has already destroyed two men he suspected of the smooch with Aphrodite. That is why she and I meet in a friend's house, and I must be stealthily coming and going. There is much gossip on the island— they are idle worthless people—you know. And if it came to the ears of this Ajax—"

"Ajax?"

"He is Aphrodite's husband—he would track me down and rip out my intestines and devour them before my eyes."

"How very disagreeable for you both. Would this Aphrodite confirm your statement, if necessary?"

"Would she fuse a bomb and take it to bed with her! No, sir. She is too afraid of Ajax. He bashes her if the dinner is late. He would grind her to powder."

"I see. Well, you spent the whole afternoon with this divine creature?"

"Sure thing."

"But you still had something in reserve, so to speak, for Mrs. Blaydon?"

"With women," announced Nikki, "I have the inexhaustible powers of Zeus the Thunderer."

"And you still claim that Mrs. Blaydon made an assignation with you for 9:15 last night, though the lecture would be over at 9:30—and her sister might be expected to return to the cabin?"

"A quarter of an hour, an hour, five hours—what does it matter?" said Nikki, in his grandest manner. "The music of love has many tempi. I will not say the ravishing Melissa made an assignation—not in so many words. But she whispered to me, yesterday morning, that she would see me before the dance, she would be waiting for me. Her eyes told me the rest."

"Including the exact time she expected you?"

"I should have gone to her cabin earlier, but I was detained."

Nigel did not think anything more could be extracted from the incorrigible Nikki, so he asked him to fetch Peter Trubody. Nigel had been sure, for some little time now, that he knew the identity of the murderer and a good deal about the circumstances of the two crimes; there was only one pattern into which the pieces would all fit. Nothing he had been told during his recent interviews disrupted this pattern. There remained Peter Trubody. Nigel felt a marked reluctance to come to grips with the young man; he had a feeling that Peter's evidence would be crucial, and a vague fear that it might explode his whole theory of the crimes; also, he found Peter a tiresome person to deal with—half boy, half man, he combined the adult male's closed-circuit mind with the irresponsibility and unpredictability of childhood.

Sighing wearily, for he was very tired by now, Nigel went out on deck to let the sea breeze refresh him. The coastline of the mainland was just visible, far ahead. In two hours' time, or three, the *Menelaos* would be docking. It would be a feat to have solved the mystery and handed over the murderer within the space of fourteen hours; but Nigel felt no gratification at the idea.

The salt wind buzzed in his ears. Tappings and cracklings from the wireless officer's room reminded him that all depended upon the message from Kalymnos awaited there. Smoke was uncoiling fatly from the single funnel and streaming backward over the ship's white wake. The sun, almost at meridian, hurt the eye as its light ricocheted off the dancing waves and the brass fittings on the bridge deck.

Peter Trubody's head came into view, as he climbed the ladder from the boat deck, Nikki behind him.

XII

"Do you smoke?"

"Thanks. I'm not in training." The boy's hand shook as he lit the cigarette Nigel offered.

"I've got about as far as I can with this investigation. It's just a matter now of fitting in a few odd pieces."

"You mean, you're going to have someone arrested?"

"I suppose so."

"For killing that—that vile woman?"

"A child was killed too."

"Oh, I know. I'm not condoning it."

A spasm of irritation shook Nigel. Who the hell was this callow, pompous youth to condone or not to condone?

"You wanted Miss Ambrose dead. You think you've got what you wanted. All right. Why go on being vindictive about her?"

"Did you ask me up here to deliver a moral discourse?"

"No. I asked you because I must know what it was you saw on Kalymnos which gave you such a shock."

"And I've already told you, it's nothing to do with the case."

"Peter, who are you protecting? Faith?"

"Faith! Good Lord, no!" The boy had said it too quickly and, as if aware of having given something away, went on with a show of anger, "And I'll trouble you to keep my sister's name out of this."

Nigel sighed. "I'm trying to treat you as a reasonable human being. But if you will talk like the clean-limbed young misunderstood hero in an Edwardian melodrama, we shall get nowhere."

Peter Trubody flushed. He was still sensitive to ridicule.

"Two people," Nigel went on, "have told me that you appeared to be in a bad way yesterday afternoon. Mr. Chalmers, and Mrs. Blaydon—if you'll allow me to mention *her* name."

Peter again flushed angrily; then, becoming aware of the friendly smile with which Nigel had accompanied those last eight words, attempted a smile himself. Nigel said:

"I don't have to be a mind reader to know about your feelings for Melissa or to guess that it is she you are trying to protect. I admire you for it, but I think you're going the wrong way about it."

"Perhaps I'm the best judge of that." Peter Trubody had not got the stiffness out of his voice yet.

"Oh dear me no, you aren't. A man in love is the last person to be able to see straight."

Peter was visibly mollified by the status Nigel had given him. "But, you know, it was just something I misinterpreted."

"My point is this—you're not going the right way about things, if you withhold evidence. You don't want the Athens police to start grilling her about it, surely?"

"God, no! But they needn't—"

"I'm sorry. Either you tell me what it's all about, or I shall have to tell them it's a matter they must investigate."

So, at last, Peter Trubody yielded up his story. Yesterday afternoon he had been mooching about the island, looking for Melissa. He had tried the two main bathing beaches, unsuccessfully. He then returned to the harbor; but, not seeing her anywhere on the waterfront, he had walked out at random along the rough road which led westward. Turning a corner, he saw the Chalmerses and Primrose ahead, sauntering in the same direction. He had no wish for their company, so he clambered up the hillside to his right. Presently, he found himself on a shoulder of hill overlooking a narrow cove. On the west side of this cove he descried two figures, one of which wore a yellow bathing cap. He had found Melissa; but, as usual, the wretched Ianthe was with her.

"You're sure it *was* Ianthe?"

"Well, I suppose at that point I just assumed it was. They were quite a long way off—several hundred yards below me, I should think. It was a woman, anyway."

"So then?"

"Well, I thought I'd shove off. But I changed my mind." Peter was looking extremely shamefaced; his eyes would not meet Nigel's.

"You stayed where you were?"

"Actually, I went a bit closer—I mean, after I'd climbed away from them, up the hill, I sort of changed my mind."

"You wanted to feel you were at least near her?"

"Yes, that's it," said Peter gratefully. "I suppose I'm an awful fool about her, but—"

"I understand."

Nigel thought he understood only too well. The boy had hoped to watch Melissa sunbathing, Melissa naked.

"I thought it'd be fun to sort of stalk them—you know, see how near I could get without their seeing me. I made a detour. It took quite a time, because I had to be careful they didn't hear me either—there are so many loose stones on the hillside you could dislodge. Well, I got to where I could see them again, from a different angle."

A very curious expression came over the boy's face; rather like the inward, stilled look on a child's when it is about to be sick.

"And you saw—?" Nigel prompted.

"Oh, it's too ridiculous. Melissa let her head fall on the rock, I thought she was dead of course but it was just a faint or sunstroke or something." It all came out in a rush. "Melissa told me during the dance—"

"Oi, oi! Let's get this in some sort of order. Have a cigarette."

The boy was trembling like a foal. Nigel's calm voice gentled and restrained him. Helped out by Nigel's questions, the gist of Peter's evidence was as follows:

He had seen the two sisters at the sea's edge. He was about a hundred yards away, above and to one side of them. Ianthe was lying sprawled on a flat rock half in the water—he recognized her by the dull-colored skirt and jumper she wore. Melissa, naked except for the yellow bathing cap, was leaning over Ianthe, in profile to him, and appeared to be doing something to her sister's neck. Ianthe's head was raised; then Melissa let it drop back onto the rock. It was this, evidently, which had scared the boy. He had taken to his heels and scrambled up the hillside again, not once looking back. It had preyed on his mind so much that later, at the dance, he blurted out to Melissa what he had seen. The explanation she gave completely reassured him. She had been sunbathing, had gone to sleep, and woken up to find Ianthe looking queer. She tried to help her sister into a patch of shade. Ianthe fainted, collapsing onto the rock where Peter had seen her. Melissa splashed water over Ianthe's face; then, with the vague idea that one "loosened the patient's clothing" under such circumstances, tried to take off a rather tight neckband Ianthe was wearing. To get at the knot, she had to lift her sister's head, which slipped in her hand as she removed the neckband and fell back on the rock.

"But why did all this give you such a turn?"

"Frankly, I got the idea—well, Miss Ambrose—I thought she was dead, you see," Peter slowly and painfully replied.

And you thought Melissa had killed her, said Nigel to himself. Gazing full at the boy, he said, "But wasn't it a very curious interpretation to put on what you were seeing? What made you jump to the conclusion she was dead?"

"Honestly, I haven't the foggiest. I agree it was quite absurd—"

"I'll tell you, then. The wish was father to the thought.

You had wanted her dead. You hated her enough, for what you believed she did to your sister, to wish her dead. So, when you saw her lying unconscious, your own unconscious instantly made the assumption."

"Do you think that's the explanation?" the boy rather pathetically asked. "I expect you're right."

"It might be. It might not. How long elapsed between the first and the second occasion you saw the sisters down below in the cove?"

"I couldn't tell you. Honestly. I'd sort of lost track of time."

"Was it hours later, or minutes?"

"I'd guess it was twenty minutes or half an hour. I'd gone back up the hill, and sat there for a while, and then I'd made this detour, moving pretty slowly."

Peter Trubody was equally unhelpful about the time when these events took place: he didn't remember much about how he had got back to the harbor. However, Mr. Chalmers' and Mrs. Blaydon's evidence fixed the time with reasonable accuracy.

"You know that wicker case Melissa carries about. Did you happen to notice it on the rocks?"

"Yes, now you mention it, I did."

"She must have been considerably taken aback when you upped at her later with your suspicions."

"Oh, she was marvelous. She didn't get angry, or laugh at me, or anything—just listened, quite seriously, to what I was saying. Of course, I didn't let out what I'd really—" The boy broke off sharply.

"What you'd really thought for a moment—that she had killed her sister?" suggested Nigel.

"I wish you wouldn't put words into my mouth," Peter replied, but wearily, not angrily. Then, after a glance at Nigel, he exclaimed, "My God! You—I believe you think she did! It's fantastic. Anyone who knows Melissa would know that. Besides, her sister wasn't—didn't disappear till last night."

Nigel made no comment on this outburst. Instead, he

asked Peter if, on his way back to the harbor, he had seen any of the other passengers. It was to avoid the chance of meeting anyone that Peter had returned along the hillside instead of using the track. He had seen nobody, he said, till he reached the outskirts of the town. At one point, passing a ruined cottage, he noticed a haversack and two books lying on the ground outside it, but their owner was not in sight.

"Did you look at the books?"

"I did just glance, actually. They were lying open."

"What were they?"

"Oh, one was a Greek text—Homer. And the other looked like a commentary of some kind. It was a new book. Someone mugging up their classics. Now what have I said?"

Nigel's eyes were lit up with excitement. "Of course. I should have guessed it. You didn't recognize the haversack, I suppose?"

"No. . . . They all look alike to me."

"It could have been Mr. Street's?"

"I dare say."

"Well, returning to your own Odyssey, when you reached port, you did not return to the ship at once."

"No."

"You saw a lot of the passengers embark then. Did any of them strike you as looking disturbed, behaving in a peculiar way?"

"No. But I wasn't taking much notice."

"Did Miss Ambrose look ill, or had she recovered?"

"I didn't see her."

"Whom did you see?"

"Oh, the Chalmerses. And Jeremy Street. And the Bishop and his wife. Lots of people I don't know by name."

"Bentinck-Jones?"

"I don't remember him."

"Nikki?"

"Yes. He was there."

Nigel gazed non-committally at the boy. "Why did you nearly miss the boat yourself?"

"Can't you guess?"

"You were waiting for Melissa?"

"Yes. I just wanted to make sure she—she was all right."

"And was she?"

"Well, of course. Oh, you mean her ankle? Yes, she came hobbling along. So I was able to do something for her—you know, help her into the boat, and so forth."

A dreamy look came into Peter's eyes.

"But you didn't talk to her then, about what you'd seen?"

"Well, no. She was in pain. And one of the boatmen might have known some English. Actually, she didn't seem to want to talk, either."

"I'm most grateful to you, Peter." Nigel studied the boy's face, thin, lightly tanned, unformed as yet, sullen and defensive no longer. At this moment, the resemblance to Faith was very marked. Brother and sister shared, too, a certain wildness, recklessness of disposition, which in Peter's case was overlaid by the conventionality of school and class. Overlaid, but not buried. Faith would go all out for what she wanted, with few inhibitions or qualms of conscience, whereas Peter's idealism, synthetic though it might be, would compel a more devious approach; he was probably capable of being no less ruthless, self-centered, ambitious than his sister, than a good many people of his age, but he would have to fake up moral sanctions for immoral actions. He was a more vulnerable character than Faith, Nigel judged, and one whom certain kinds of hurt could spoil for life.

"I'm afraid," Nigel went on, "you may be in for a pretty hard knock before long. Don't let it make you lose faith in—"

Nigel was interrupted by the sudden entry of Nikki, who burst out, before Nigel could stop him, with "They've found her body! Message just come through from Kalymnos. On the seashore, near—"

"Nikki! Pipe down! We have company."

But Peter Trubody was staring aghast at the cruise manager, his lips gone white. "Whose body?" he asked in a stony voice.

"Why, Miss Ambrose's, of course. Must have been washed ashore from the ship. Got a wound in the back of the head, they say."

"For *Christ's* sake will you hold your tongue!" Nigel furiously exclaimed.

Peter Trubody's nostrils were pinched; he threw back the lock of hair that fell over his eyes, which were drenched with misery and fear.

"All right," he said. "You win. I killed her."

Elucidation

HALF AN HOUR LATER, shortly after midday, the first officer's cabin held four people. Faith Trubody sat on the bed, chewing her nails and casting covert glances at Jeremy Street, who stood looking out of the window. Nikki was shuffling through a sheaf of papers he held in his hand. Ivor Bentinck-Jones leaned against the wall near Faith, addressing an occasional remark to the girl, who hardly bothered to answer.

"What on earth does this fellow Strangeways want us here for?" Jeremy asked Nikki.

"Your guess is as good as mine, Mr. Street."

"He might at least have the good manners not to keep us waiting."

"He's been acting like Lord God Almighty," said Ivor.

"Who moves in a mysterious way his blunders to perform," Jeremy put in, with his supercilious smile. "Ah, here he is. And Mrs. Blaydon."

The door opened, the armed sailor outside saluted, and Nigel helped the limping woman into the cabin.

Bentinck-Jones hastened to offer the one available chair. She inclined her head, its profile piquant in the Indian headscarf, and rather awkwardly sat down. The four glanced at her and Nigel and one another with the uneasy neutrality of children at the start of a party.

"I've asked you here," said Nigel, "because each of you was involved, in one way or another, with the two victims of the murderer."

"Where's Peter? Why isn't Peter here?" Faith's voice was shrill.

"Peter is under close arrest. He has confessed to the crimes."

There was a dead silence, of incredulity and shock. Then Faith, whose face had gone so white that the freckles showed up like old, yellow bruise marks, cried out:

"It's a lie! I don't believe you! You never told me—"

"He has written a confession," Nigel cut in. Taking a paper from his pocket, he offered it to the girl who, without so much as glancing at it, tore it viciously into fragments.

"Here, steady on, young lady!" said Ivor.

"She's quite right," Nigel coolly remarked. "The confession is worthless."

Faith stared at him in amazement. "Then—then, why have you arrested him?"

"For his own safety. He is in danger from two people."

Jeremy Street shot a keen glance at Nigel. "You mean, there were *two* murderers?"

"No. Peter is in danger from the murderer, and from himself. He believes he knows who committed these crimes; a person he loved, as they say, not wisely but too well."

"Me?" Faith's voice was a whisper, as she stared at Nigel in horror.

"Peter is trying to protect this person. He might even kill

himself in his present state of mind, to substantiate his confession."

"Well, he's a fool then," Faith harshly exclaimed. "I told him I didn't care a damn any longer about what Miss Ambrose had done. Mrs. Blaydon, why don't *you* say something?"

"Aren't we talking at cross-purposes? Mr. Strangeways has not said it was you your brother is trying to protect."

"Quite so. But Peter also knows too much for the murderer's peace of mind. That's the other reason why I've put him under guard."

"Look here, can't you stop talking in riddles and come to the point?" said Jeremy Street. "How do you know Peter's confession was worthless, anyway?"

"You, you—! Oh, how I despise you!" Faith was glaring at the lecturer like a Fury.

"I'll give you the gist of it. You can judge for yourselves. Peter says he saw Miss Ambrose and her sister sunbathing in the cove yesterday afternoon; he was on the hillside above. Presently Miss Ambrose started walking back to the harbor alone. He ran down the hillside and interrupted her. It was only the second opportunity he'd had to talk to her alone, for she was nearly always with her sister—the first, by the way, was on Delos, when he was overheard threatening her."

"Threatening Ianthe?"

"Yes, Mrs. Blaydon. Peter says—it's quite different from the story he'd told me just before—that he interrupted Ianthe on the track, and they had a violent quarrel. She again refused to admit any of the charges he made about her treatment of his sister at school—I won't go into these now—and she said some vile and contemptuous things about Peter and his feelings for you. It was this, Peter wrote in his confession, that proved the last straw. Later, that evening, when he left the lounge to fetch something for his sister, he saw Ianthe walking along the promenade deck, forward. He followed her out onto the fo'c's'le, stunned her with a blow on the jaw, and threw her overboard. Then he noticed Primrose Chalmers watching him from the shadows, lost his head still more, strangled the child, and threw her into the swimming pool. It took only a few minutes, he says, to do this, to hurry down to the cabin, fetch his sister's stole, and return to the forward lounge. The whole thing," Nigel concluded, "leaks at every pore."

"I don't quite see that," Jeremy said.

Faith turned on him fiercely. "You wouldn't! As if Primrose would just stand watching, while Peter—"

"Exactly. But the revealing thing is the time and place of Peter's alleged crimes. He should have killed Miss Ambrose on the island, when they were quarreling and she was saying things that made him see red. If he didn't do it then, why should he do it later when he'd presumably have calmed down a bit?"

"Well, you tell us," Ivor unpleasantly remarked.

"I will." Nigel glanced around the cabin. Sitting on the bed, her legs curled beneath her, Faith Trubody was watching him fixedly, a feverish gleam in her green eyes. Jeremy Street leaned against the bulkhead on her right, jingling coins in the pocket of his royal-blue linen trousers, with the barely concealed impatience he evinced when pinned down after a lecture by some gushing member of his audience. Against the opposite wall stood Nikki, puzzled, silent, watchful; his mobile features had been responding like an actor's to each turn of the dialogue. Ivor Bentinck-Jones had plumped down on the far end of the bed from Faith; his arms were around his knees, and he regarded Nigel with the expression of a poker player ready to bluff or call a bluff.

His back to the door, Nigel glanced from one to another of them. "I certainly will," he said. "The whole, desperate object of Peter's confession was to try and divert me from the truth—the truth that Miss Ambrose was not murdered on this ship."

There were a few seconds of bewildered silence; then they all broke out together:

"But that's impossible!"

"Not on the ship! I don't understand."

"You must be crazy, Mr. Strangeways."

"When was she murdered, then?"

"But, when you told me, I assumed—"

"Yes, Mrs. Blaydon?" asked Nigel, looking at her meditatively.

"Well, that Ianthe's body had been washed ashore."

"That was what the murderer intended us to think." Nigel spoke to the four others now. "I had just been telling Mrs. Blaydon, before we came up here, that a woman's body had been found on Kalymnos. The clothing and general appearance answer to the description of Miss Ambrose which we gave the authorities on Kalymnos. The body was wedged under a rock in the cove where she and her sister bathed yesterday afternoon. There was a wound on the back of her head. I'm sorry, Mrs. Blaydon, to go over all this again."

She had buried her face in her hands.

"It seems to me a quite inexcusable proceeding on your part," said Jeremy, throwing up his head and almost neighing the words. "I cannot conceive what possible object you have in—"

"You will, in due course."

Ivor Bentinck-Jones leaned forward, his face both weary and impudent. "And how does the great detective *know* the body was not washed ashore from the ship?"

"For one thing, she did not disappear till about 9:15 P.M. The ship left Kalymnos at six. By 9:15 we'd be some sixty miles from the island. Drowned bodies do not rise to the surface again for several days. It is almost impossible, the Captain tells me, that wind and current should drive a submerged body sixty miles between 9:15 P.M., when we were notified of Miss Ambrose's disappearance, and 11:35 this morning, when her body was found."

"Oh, *almost* impossible?" said Ivor, looking around at the others for applause, as though he had scored a point.

"I'm very stupid, I wasn't awfully well last night, but I

can't understand how my sister *could* have been killed anywhere else—I mean, she was on the ship, you've said so yourself, till 9:15."

"A woman, who was *taken* to be your sister, was seen for a short while at the lecture. It was pretty dark up there, though. Identities can be mistaken. All people can be impersonated. Nikki has questioned the quartermaster who was receiving the landing tickets as the passengers re-embarked. The sailor was shown the passport photograph of Miss Ambrose, and he has no recollection of her returning to the ship."

"He could easily have missed her," protested Jeremy. "Have you checked the number of landing cards handed back?"

"Of course. The same number were returned as were handed out in the morning."

"Well, then."

"The person who murdered Miss Ambrose must have handed in two cards, one stuck to the other so that the sailor thought he was being given a single one."

"Have you any proof of this?" asked Ivor with a sneer.

"No."

Jeremy tossed up his head again. "You're simply wasting our time, with a lot of grotesque theories that—"

"I agree, it would save time if the murderer confessed." Nigel gazed hard at Jeremy Street. "Now, according to your story, Mrs. Blaydon—"

"I do hope you know what you're saying, Mr. Strangeways. But haven't you forgotten that I saw Ianthe before the lecture? I took her some fruit just after dinner. I'm quite sure it was she, not someone impersonating her."

"We've only your word for it that she was in the cabin at all."

The familiar laugh came bubbling out. "But, my *dear* Mr. Strangeways, why should I say she was there if she wasn't?"

"You'd have to say it, if it was you who later impersonated Ianthe at the lecture."

Looking around at the others, she made a fluttering, helpless gesture. I must be dreaming. This is all absolutely mad."

"And after all," Nigel pursued, "who could impersonate your sister so successfully as yourself?"

"My dear sir," exclaimed Nikki, "there's no resemblance between them at all! How can you suggest it? A beautiful creature, a veritable naiad, and—"

"Miss Massinger is a sculptor. The first time she saw Mrs. Blaydon and her sister, she commented on their likeness to each other—in bone structure, figure, and so on. None of us has seen Mrs. Blaydon without her make-up. And the Bishop of Solway told me how alike the sisters were as small girls."

"This whole conversation seems to me quite unreal. I don't see why I should go on humoring your extraordinary fancies, Mr. Strangeways."

"You are perfectly at liberty to leave," Nigel answered.

The woman shrugged; then, in her deep, husky voice said, almost on a note of gaiety, "No, I think I'll stay. I can't resist the temptation to discover where this nonsense is leading."

She spoke for the others, too, whether or not she knew it; it was as though Nigel had presented them with a fantastic cocoon of paradox and unreality, and they must wait to see what emerged when he unwound it.

"What you seem to be implying, Mr. Strangeways, is that I murdered my sister."

Nigel said nothing, but watched her averted head.

"You're saying," she persisted, "that she was impersonated. Obviously whoever impersonated her was the murderer—according to your theory."

"No. It's not 'obviously.' Let us suppose you impersonated her in order to protect somebody else, to give him —the murderer—an alibi."

"Who would the murderer be, then, that I'm supposed to have been protecting?" she asked, in the brisk, emotionless tone of a nurse humoring a lunatic.

"Oh, I can do that one," put in Bentinck-Jones. "If we're playing this as a parlor game, the answer is our respected savant, Mr. Jeremy Street."

"What the devil do you mean by that?" exclaimed Jeremy.

"You are the only one of us who has a perfect alibi for the time when Miss Ambrose was *supposed* to have committed suicide or been murdered. You were lecturing," said Ivor, beaming at his companions.

Jeremy Street gave a contemptuous sniff. "This is becoming quite farcical. You seem to be leaving that wretched child out of account altogether—or are you going to tell us that Primrose as well as Miss Ambrose was killed on the island?"

"I'll come to her later," said Nigel. "Mr. Street, you told me that, when you went ashore again yesterday afternoon, you spent the whole time reading. On a hillside west of the harbor. You never moved from the spot?"

"That is so."

"Peter Trubody found your books and your haversack there; but you were not in sight. So you did move from the spot."

Jeremy Street shook his head, like a horse tormented by flies. "Oh, I dare say I did get up for a minute or two—to stretch my legs."

"And it was not a detective novel you were reading."

"I fail to see what concern of yours my personal reading is."

"What *is* all this about?" said Faith Trubody. She was watching Jeremy's discomfiture with curiosity and a kind of covert glee.

"In a nutshell," said Nigel, "Mr. Street had a strong motive for killing Ianthe Ambrose: he could have seen her, from where he sat, walking along the track—according to Mrs. Blaydon's statement, her sister started back toward the harbor, alone, at about 4:45. He could have run down the hill, intercepted her, struck her on the back of the head, and thrown the body into the sea. The body might later have been washed ashore where it was found. Any comments, Mr. Street?"

"One doesn't comment on a tissue of falsehood, like—"

"Falsehood? Why did you tell me you were reading a detective novel, and that you never moved from the spot?"

"I did not kill Miss Ambrose." The lecturer's voice went a little high.

"I know you didn't. You are not the type to kill on the spur of the moment; and you could not have known beforehand that you would have the opportunity yesterday afternoon. You had a different plan for Miss Ambrose, I suggest."

."This is pernicious nonsense."

"Connected with what you were reading on the hillside."

Jeremy Street gave him a furious look, and made for the door. The armed sailor outside stopped him, but at a sign from Nigel let him go.

Nigel had little doubt about the reason for Jeremy's evasions. Earlier yesterday, Faith had refused the man's offer of marriage. This blow to his vanity, together with the blackmailing attempt of Bentinck-Jones, had determined him to get his own back on Ianthe, the original source of his troubles. He would make sure that, this time, Ianthe should not humiliate him during a lecture; more than this, he might turn the tables on her. No doubt he had been mugging up the text and consulting the new commentary which Peter had seen, with the view of laying some trap into which Ianthe could be drawn, if and when she took the offensive at the lecture. A practiced lecturer can nearly always make a questioner from the audience look foolish. To humiliate Ianthe in public would be a great satisfaction in itself; to vindicate his own scholarship against Ianthe's would also re-establish his status with Mr. Trubody, whose financial backing Jeremy needed. The whole plan was, of course, childish, petty, undignified—but just the sort of thing a vain exhibitionist like Jeremy would find appealing, and would hate to have exposed. Hence Jeremy's discomposure when Nigel first asked him what he had been reading, and the lie about a detective novel; as for his saying he never left the spot, it was probable that Jeremy Street had genuinely forgotten he had done so.

Nigel had no wish for Street to be further humiliated. Brushing aside a rather avid question from Faith, he said, "There is no link between Street and Mrs. Blaydon, therefore no reason why she should have impersonated her sister to protect him."

The woman at the table sighed wearily. "I do wish you would get this idea out of your head."

"You must bear with me a little longer." Nigel gave her a veiled look, then addressed the others as if she were not there. "On the theory that it was Mrs. Blaydon who did the impersonation, it might have been as a willing accessory or an unwilling one. Which brings us to you, Nikki."

The cruise manager started convulsively. *"Me?* Have you gone crackers?" He threw away the toothpick he had been at work with, and took two steps toward Nigel.

"Your alibi for yesterday afternoon—"

"Now take it easy, Mr. Strangeways, take it easy! That was confidential. You know? Top secret."

"Will the person you were with confirm your alibi? And how would I know it was not a put-up job between you both?"

"But say, I thought you believed me!"

"Will the Athens police believe you? It could look bad for you. You are known to have told Mrs. Blaydon privately about a special bathing place. You tell none of the other passengers. It sounds like an assignation, doesn't it? You go along there—Miss Massinger and I saw you creeping off in a highly furtive way. But, when you arrive, you find Miss Ambrose there too. There's a quarrel. Miss Ambrose insults you. You see red and hit her—a little too hard. The body has to be disposed of. Wedge it under a rock; it's likely that Miss Ambrose was murdered where her body has been found. You and Mrs. Blaydon then make a plan, to create the illusion that her sister was killed, or committed suicide, on the ship. You're in a better position than anyone to fiddle the landing tickets. Your liaison with Mrs. Blaydon—"

"*Please!* I find this absolutely indecent."

"You are quite at liberty to go, Mrs. Blaydon," said Nigel, for the second time.

"Are you suggesting that I—I became an accomplice in my sister's murder, because of an—an attachment to this man?"

"The fun gets fast and furious," said Ivor with a malicious chuckle.

"Hold your tongue, you goddam heel!" shouted Nikki.

"It's a line the police might work on," said Nigel coolly. "We must have all noticed how attentive and solicitous Mrs. Blaydon was toward her sister. Which makes it all the odder that she should have allowed her to walk back alone to the harbor after an attack of sunstroke."

"I did explain that to you. You've no idea how obstinate poor Ianthe could be."

"I must admit," said Nigel, "I cannot see Mrs. Blaydon *willingly* co-operating with her sister's murderer."

"Not for a man she'd fallen for?" Ivor outrageously asked. "The way these two carried on in public—"

"We know you are a keen student of human behavior," said Nigel, raising his voice to quell the outbreak which Bentinck-Jones's remark produced. "And we know why. If Mrs. Blaydon was an *un*willing accessory, we don't have to look far for the murderer."

"This time, there are witnesses to what you're saying. Defamation of character is actionable. Watch your step."

"Well, I'll say it," cried Faith Trubody. "I don't care a damn. You tried to blackmail Jeremy. You're a blackmailer, you fat little reptile. You blackmailed Mrs. Blaydon into impersonating her sister. Isn't that what you mean, Mr. Strangeways?"

"Any comments?" asked Nigel, looking fixedly at Ivor.

"My solicitor will make all the comments that are necessary."

"I really wouldn't start invoking the law, if I were you. Mrs. Blaydon, what hold did this man have on you?"

"None. I keep telling you, you're under a ridiculous misconception—it's absurd, mad."

"Are you a heavy sleeper, may I ask?"

"I really can't see—yes, I am rather."

"You told me you slept for a while yesterday afternoon in the cove. When you woke up, you found your sister was looking ill. Are you sure she was alive?"

"Of course she was alive." The beautiful eyes opened wide. "Oh, you're thinking Mr. Bentinck-Jones might have killed her while I was asleep, crept up and stunned her from behind before she could cry out and wake me?"

"Peter Trubody told me he'd seen you both from the hillside and had thought your sister was dead."

"Oh, I know. Silly boy. I explained it to him at the dance. Poor Ianthe had fainted, and I clumsily let her head fall back on the rock. But it wasn't a serious knock she got—not enough to cause a wound—oh, I see, you're wondering if it was an accident and I lost my head and told lies about it." The woman, who had talked till now in a slow, almost dragging way, as if still exhausted, brought out these last words with a rush.

"It's a pity," said Nigel. "For, as far as I can see, Bentinck-Jones had an extremely strong motive for murdering Primrose Chalmers."

"Oh, it's Primrose now, is it?" said Ivor.

"Yes. If one thing in this case is clear, it's that the murderer believed Primrose had seen the murder being done."

"B-but, you said it was *not* done on the ship," stammered Nikki.

"It wasn't. Primrose was spying on Miss Ambrose while she was sunbathing in the cove. She wrote down in her notebook what she'd seen. When her body was found, the notebook was not in her sporran, where she always kept it, nor in her cabin. Bentinck-Jones finally admitted to me that he'd stolen the notebook—off the body, he said. The ink had run, he said, and was indecipherable. Only the last entry, written in pencil, was legible."

"But I told you," Ivor broke in, mopping his brow. "I told you what she'd written. It was nothing to do with seeing Miss Ambrose murdered."

"You told me, under strong pressure. But how do I know you told me the truth? You admitted you had taken the notebook. You led us to assume you'd taken it off the child's body. Very clever. But suppose you'd taken it from her while she was alive, and found she'd been an eyewitness of what you did on the island. You had the notebook, but the knowledge was still in the child's head. So she had to be silenced for good and all. Naturally, when I questioned you this morning, you'd make up a false version of what she wrote."

"You bloody double-crosser!" Ivor muttered, hunched up, glaring at Nigel.

"Why should anyone murder the child except to suppress evidence? Who knew that this evidence existed, in her notebook, except you? You're properly dished, aren't you?"

"And don't forget," Faith broke in excitedly, "I saw him following Primrose out toward the swimming pool last night."

"And another witness saw Primrose, just before, moving in the same direction with a woman the witness took to be Ianthe Ambrose. I must ask you again, Mrs. Blaydon, did this man have some hold on you and force you to pose as your sister?"

She trailed a languid hand across her brow. "And I must tell you again, he didn't."

"Very well," said Nigel after a pause. "We'll drop the idea of forced collusion on your part. But I'm afraid this will open up a still less inviting prospect. Let us assume for the moment that Bentinck-Jones did not kill Miss Ambrose, and that his account of what Primrose wrote in her notebook was true."

Nigel moved over to the door, cast a glance around the

four in the cabin, and took a sheet of paper from his pocket. The cabin had grown unpleasantly warm; there was a prickle of sweat on Faith's forehead, at the roots of her blond hair, and Ivor was mopping his face again. Nikki's dark skin gleamed, like polished wood. The three of them looked all at sea, like survivors in an open boat drifting without sails or oars, whither they knew not and were past caring.

Nigel opened the sheet of paper. "This is what Primrose saw. A wicker case floating out from under the rocks, and the arm and head of a swimmer retrieving it." He paused. The silence protracted itself. Then Faith exclaimed, "What is it, Mrs. Blaydon? Are you feeling—?"

"Is that *all* she saw?"

"Absolutely all, Mrs. Blaydon," said Nigel.

She was sitting in a curiously rigid pose; then she gave herself a sort of angry shake. "Well then, what's all the fuss about?"

"Primrose thought the person she saw swimming was Ianthe. The swimmer had a dark head—looked like a seal, she says—and was not wearing a bathing cap. Mrs. Blaydon always wore a yellow one. But Ianthe had always said she couldn't swim. Primrose had it in for Ianthe, and believed she'd caught her out lying. Mrs. Blaydon, you never told me about the wicker case floating away."

"My good man, one can't always remember everything," the woman replied, with an edge on her voice.

"When did this happen?"

"Just before Ianthe fainted. As I told you, I tried to get her into some shade. In doing so, I accidentally kicked the case off a rock into the water."

"Then she fainted?"

"Yes."

"But, instead of reviving her, you swam out to retrieve the case?"

"I retrieved it in order to revive her. There was a bottle of smelling salts in it."

"I see."

"And I was in such a hurry that I did not put on my bathing cap. Does that set your mind at ease?"

Nigel studied the sheet of paper again. "Primrose was almost certain the swimmer had been Ianthe. She went off and made a plan to confirm it. This plan was the cause of her death; I'll come back to it presently. First, let me reconstruct the murder in the cove." Nigel was now addressing the other three again, as if the fourth person were not present. "Mrs. Blaydon stuns her sister with a heavy stone—"

"Say! You're crazy!" Nikki expostulated. "On the beach there, where anyone might have seen her?"

"She and her sister had been there for an hour or two— long enough to discover what a deserted place it is. The only people who turned up were the Chalmerses, whom Ianthe got rid of double-quick, very conveniently for her sister. They were at the water's edge, screened from the track on one side by a steep overhang and by boulders."

"But anyone approaching from the eastward side could have seen them," said Nikki. "You come around a jutting bit of hillside, along the track from the harbor, and you look straight across the cove—"

"You seem to know it very well, Nikki."

The cruise manager gave Nigel an angry look, and took refuge in silence.

"The fact is that, on that stony track, people couldn't walk silently. You'd hear footsteps before they came around the escarpment. Sound travels far in the Greek air. As I was saying, Mrs. Blaydon stuns her sister; then she drags her into the water and wedges the body under a rock. It was all over in a minute. She could not know that Peter Trubody was watching from the hillside."

Faith Trubody's breath came out in a hiss.

"Peter saw Ianthe, stretched out on a rock at the water's edge. He saw Mrs. Blaydon, naked except for the bathing cap, lift her sister's head and let it drop back with a crack onto the rock. Mrs. Blaydon had just struck her and was making sure she was unconscious. Peter got the impression

Ianthe was dead—she was, all but. This gave him a terrible shock, and he ran away without looking behind him. He got this shock because, though he'd not seen it happening, some instinct told him that Mrs. Blaydon was responsible for Ianthe's death. He could not bear to stay a moment longer. Had he done so, he would have observed Mrs. Blaydon pull her sister's body into the water and wedge it under a rock, where nobody passing along the track could see it. In doing this, her bathing cap got pulled off. When she came out of the water, she noticed that her dress and the wicker case had fallen in. The latter was floating away. She dived in, without putting on her cap again, because it was vital to her plan that the case should not be lost. In the case was Ianthe's landing card."

The woman's eyes, perplexed now and troubled, met Nigel's again.

"You mustn't say these horrible things. It's frightening."

"Having disposed of the body, retrieved the case and the wet dress, Mrs. Blaydon put on her bathrobe and moved around to the other side of the cove, where she could dry her dress in the sun. Mr. Chalmers found her there half an hour or so later. He told me, by the way, that 'her bathing things and dress were *spread out to dry* on the rocks'—an interesting, unconscious assumption, for he could hardly have seen, from the track above, that the dress was wet. In spite of Mr. Chalmers warning her that it was getting late, Mrs. Blaydon still nearly missed the ship. Didn't you?"

"I hurt my ankle. That's what made me late."

"Mrs. Blaydon *had* to be as late as possible. If she arrived on board at the very last minute, there was every chance that, in the general bustle and sensation of her arrival, she'd be able to palm Ianthe's landing ticket together with her own onto the quarter-master. She succeeded. There would now be evidence that Ianthe had returned to the ship. And it was most important there should be; otherwise, if the rest of Mrs. Blaydon's plan went wrong, the investigation would discover that no one in fact had seen

Ianthe walking back along the track, or at the quayside, or returning to the *Menelaos.*"

Nigel was certainly gripping his audience now. It was as though they felt that, after turning them down several blind alleys, he was now leading them along an open road. Like a jury returning to give a verdict of Guilty, they kept their eyes averted from the woman in the dock. Nikki seemed on the point of expostulating, but so much out of his depth that he could not do so. Bentinck-Jones had relaxed, and was eying Nigel with an expression half skeptical, half respectful. Faith Trubody, who had been seized by a fit of nervous yawning, fidgeted, bit her nails, ran her fingers through her blond hair. As for the woman Nigel was accusing now, the deepening anxiety in her eyes and the tense pose of her body showed the strain under which she labored. There was a loud bellow from the *Menelaos'* steam whistle, and she visibly flinched.

"Are we coming in?" Faith gave a nervous laugh. "We must be nearly there."

Nigel resumed, speaking faster. "Mrs. Blaydon is seen at dinner, alone. She tells us she's taking some fruit to Ianthe in the cabin, and Ianthe is feeling better and will attend the lecture. After dinner, Mrs. Blaydon is at the bar for a little, then retires 'to dress for the dance.' She goes to her cabin, removes her make-up, puts on her sister's clothes. Remember, no one saw the two sisters *together* after they'd been seen in the cove. Posing as Ianthe, Mrs. Blaydon goes to the lecture; she behaves in such a way—sighing heavily and muttering to herself—that afterward people would accept Ianthe's disappearance as suicide. Ianthe, we were meant to think, threw herself off the ship. With any luck at all, the body would not be discovered in the cove for several days at least—long enough to sustain the idea that it had been driven back to the island by current and wind. But it was at this point that Primrose Chalmers' plan cut across the murderer's.

"Primrose got up, when 'Ianthe' left the lecture, followed her down to the promenade deck, caught up with her, and, according to one eyewitness, took hold of her sleeve, spoke to her, wouldn't let go. 'Miss Ambrose,' this witness told us, 'went stiff and tried to pull her arm away as though she wanted to go down to her cabin.' She did, of course—very badly; one sister must disappear now, and the other return to her own identity. But Primrose said something to 'Ianthe' which made her change her mind. There can be little doubt what it was: Primrose hinted that she had seen something peculiar in the cove that afternoon.

"All Primrose wanted, of course, was to confirm her belief that Ianthe had been lying when she said she couldn't swim. She took the woman she believed to be Ianthe out onto the fo'c's'le, under the pretext of requiring privacy, maneuvered her to the swimming pool, and pushed her in."

"I happened at that moment to be at an open window in the saloon. I heard a faint cry and a splash. Then, seconds later, the sounds were repeated. This is what happened— Primrose stayed on the edge of the pool, to see if the woman could swim. She could. She swam a few strokes, seized the child's ankles, dragged her in, and strangled her. We don't know just what Primrose had said to her on the way to the pool; but it was enough to convince her—quite mistakenly, as it happened—that the child had witnessed the murder in the cove.

"Another witness saw a woman she took to be Miss Ambrose hurrying down toward her cabin, with a rug draped over her head. The murderer had snatched it up from a deck chair on the way back from the pool, to conceal her dripping hair and clothes. It is now just before 9:15—five minutes since 'Ianthe' left the lecture."

"Wait a minute," interrupted Ivor. "Surely someone would have noticed a trail of moisture on the stairway or the corridor?"

"Not necessarily. The carpeting is a dark color. You yourself were too busy spying on Nikki to notice the carpeting;

Nikki had his mind on the assignation, and then on the unexpected reception he had got. Other passengers *might* have noticed. But they'd not see anything unusual in it—people are constantly running from the swimming pool or the showers to their cabins, still wet. Well, then. Nikki enters Mrs. Blaydon's cabin. I won't go into this in detail; but he finds a woman there, naked, her body wet, her hair soaking. She has just had time to tear off her wet clothes. Mrs. Blaydon has tried to explain this by saying she'd taken a shower before dressing for the dance. I am asked to believe that a woman of fashion, a woman who always wore a bathing cap in the sea, would go under a shower just before a dance without any covering for her hair.

"After Nikki leaves her cabin, she dresses and puts on her make-up again, to appear at the dance, as Melissa, some twenty minutes later. It was a quick change. She did not have time to dry her hair properly, so she sprayed it with oil—Peter Trubody commented on this during the dance —to account for its looking wet. One must admire the attention to detail, at such a nerve-racking—"

"Stop! This is insane! I've just thought of something. It proves I didn't—couldn't impersonate Ianthe. My ankle. *She* wasn't limping when she was seen at the lecture, was she? or on the deck afterward? I'd hurt my ankle. I couldn't possibly have walked without a limp. Could I?"

"Sure, sure!" Nikki excitedly spoke. "I guess that proves the lady is innocent."

Nigel gazed meditatively at her face, anxious and distorted beneath the heavy make-up. "I'm afraid not. Miss Ambrose had a rather ungainly way of walking. Mrs. Blaydon's ankle was not badly sprained, only a bit swollen. She could walk on it, given a little resolution, so as not to betray a limp. She could even have turned her ankle deliberately, in order to give the effect of Ianthe's awkward gait."

Nikki's face was crestfallen. Faith chewed her nails. Ivor had the gloating look of one who has witnessed a murderous counterpunch in the boxing ring.

"No," said Nigel slowly, "that one won't wash. There's a

far better reason why Mrs. Blaydon could not have murdered her sister."

"Well, for God's sake!" exclaimed Ivor.

"She *didn't?*" Faith said, on a rush of pent-up breath.

"The theory I have outlined to you," went on Nigel impassively, "is a very attractive one. In fact, it had been in my mind from early on, and each new fact I discovered could be fitted into it. It covers all the facts, but one."

"Yes?" The woman in the chair breathed it rather than spoke it.

"Mrs. Blaydon had no possible, conceivable *motive* for murdering her sister."

"How do you know?" snarled Bentinck-Jones.

"You say she is innocent?" Nikki asked, in an ominously quiet voice.

"Mrs. Blaydon is innocent."

"Well, then," said Faith indignantly, "why all this—this rigmarole, like the end of a corny detective novel?"

"I rather agree, Faith; you've—er 'said it,' " murmured the husky voice, wryly stressing the colloquialism.

"Yes, Goddammit, why did we have to have this circus? —torturing her, making us all think—"

"I thought you knew Mrs. Blaydon," Nigel cut in harshly.

"Knew her?" Nikki looked stupid, stunned.

"Well enough to know she wasn't the kind of woman who'd kill anyone."

"Oh, so that's it," Bentinck-Jones sneered. "She didn't murder because she's not a murdering type. God preserve us from amateur detectives!"

Nigel ignored him. After one glance at the drooping shoulders, the relaxed, exhausted pose, of the woman in the chair, who had closed her eyes and was smiling faintly at last, he turned away.

"And now we come to Miss Trubody. We have not yet dealt with her."

"Me?" The girl jerked upright, as if every nerve in her body had suddenly been alerted. The bridge telegraph clanged twice. Through the window the heads of ship cranes could be seen, stalking slowly past. The engines of the *Menelaos* thumped as the screws were reversed.

"Me?" cried Faith, white-faced, her thin body tensed.

"Mrs. Blaydon," said Nigel, "I'm afraid this has been an ordeal for you. I'll spare you the rest. Nikki, will you take her to her cabin, please?"

The woman rose, glanced at the others with unseeing eyes, smiled uncertainly at no one in particular, and with Nikki's hand under her elbow limped toward the door. She was within a yard of it when, in a quiet, conversational tone, Faith Trubody said,

"Oh, Brossy. Could you—"

The woman stopped, swung around involuntarily; and it was, unmistakably, the movement of a schoolmistress who, at the blackboard, hears from behind her some noise of mischief or impertinence, some whisper or rustle or giggle, and swings around to quell it. She knew at once she had betrayed herself—before any of the others but Nigel realized it. The exquisitely, heavily made-up face altered before their eyes, working, distorting itself, shifting, coarsening, the mask of Melissa shaling away as when a landslide slowly erases the features of a cliff, and Ianthe Ambrose's face, Ianthe's personality were unbared from beneath. The make-up was still there, but it could no longer hold together the fiction that this was Melissa Blaydon.

They all perceived it now. Ianthe could see her self-betrayal in their eyes. She did not even try to bluff it out. Instinct took over—the blind, furious instinct for self-preservation. She had the door open, shaking off Nikki's hand. The armed sailor outside barred her way, and she clawed at his face so that he reeled back, blood starting from a furrow under his eye. She ran to the rail, saw concrete quayside, not yielding water, far beneath; darted away aft, down the ladder to the boat deck, across the deck to the starboard side, but the rail here was lined with passengers, who turned like sheep when they heard Nikki's shouts of "Stop her! Stop that woman!" But, before they had assembled their wits, Ianthe was down on the promenade deck, moving aft again, with that crippled, scurrying, lurching gait, the headscarf streaming out behind her.

From the boat deck aft, Nikki hailed a group of sailors on the poop deck below. Four of them began to run forward, two on either side of the ship. Ianthe saw them coming, as she reached the engine-room hatch. The hatch was open. Thirty feet below, the turbines, bedded in the ship's floor, gleamed with oily sweat. Ianthe Ambrose had scuffled herself over the combing of the hatch before the sailors could reach her or any of the passengers crowded along the rail had realized what was amiss. She fell headfirst among the turbines, a long scream trailing behind her. The yellow scarf came fluttering to rest over her shattered head.

II

"So you thought I was carrying on like a corny detective novel?" said Nigel, gazing at Faith Trubody with mock severity.

The girl wriggled in her deck chair. "Well, all that phony business of pinning the crime on each suspect in turn—you know—in the last chapter. I must say, though, when you turned on me at the end I nearly jumped out of my skin. I thought for a second I must be the murderer, instead of remembering it was my entrance cue." She turned to her brother. "Mr. Strangeways told me, before the meeting, that at some point he'd say, 'and now we come to Miss Trubody'; that was to be the signal. Then, just as Mrs. Blaydon was going out, I had to say something to her bringing in Miss Ambrose's nickname—I mean, I still thought it was Mrs. Blaydon. That's how we caught her out."

"Don't gloat, twin," said Peter repressively.

"I'm not gloating. And anyway, she deserved everything she got."

"Oh, you young creatures and your facile moral judgments!" Clare lazily drawled. "I suppose it was one of your nerve wars, Nigel."

"You suppose right. She might still have got away with it, even then. That's why I faked up a case against each of the others, and then came to the case against Melissa Blaydon, which was the strongest of all. I had to keep Ianthe on tenterhooks and gradually screw up the tension, hoping that when it was suddenly relaxed she'd be off her guard for a minute and give herself away."

"It must have been hell for her, after taking us in that she was Melissa, to find that you could prove Melissa guilty," said Faith.

"Yes. Particularly when I was reconstructing, with almost every detail correct, how *Ianthe* had in fact committed the crimes."

"A sort of mirror image, you mean?" said Clare. "Ianthe had killed Melissa and Primrose, and was successfully impersonating her sister, and now she found you apparently had a watertight case against Melissa for killing Primrose and Ianthe? She couldn't extricate herself from the toils, except by admitting she was Ianthe, which would be as good as confessing that she'd murdered Melissa. Very awkward for her."

"As I say, she might have got away with it if she'd just sat tight. But the sudden relaxing of tension when I said Melissa was innocent—that was too much for her."

"I can't understand why she stayed on in the cabin—when you were accusing everyone in turn," said Faith. "Surely she'd be afraid of saying something that gave her away."

"She didn't dare leave. You remember, I told her twice she was at liberty to go. If she'd been innocent, she'd have left. But she had to know just how much I knew, or guessed, of the truth. And she kept her nerve remarkably well. It wasn't till I suddenly relaxed the tension that she gave herself away—twice."

"Twice?" asked Faith.

"Yes, after you addressed her as 'Brossy,' of course—but, before that, when you upbraided me for behaving like a corny detective novel, she said—do you remember?—'I

rather agree, Faith; you've—er—said it.' She put the colloquialism in quotes, as a rather pedantic schoolmistress
would when talking to a pupil. Melissa would never have
used a slang expression self-consciously like that."

The four were sitting on the boat deck of the *Menelaos*,
which was steaming eastward again. The formalities at
Athens had taken little more than twenty-four hours,
thanks mainly to the long statement made by Nigel to the
police authorities; he would have to return later, when the
results of the autopsy on Primrose Chalmers were known
and the body of Melissa Blaydon had been conveyed from
Kalymnos to Athens. Legal identification of the two sisters'
bodies could only be proved when reports from their den-
tists came to hand; but the authorities had no doubt that
Nigel's solution of the mystery was broadly correct. So the
Menelaos, after oiling, was allowed to resume her cruise.
Nearly all the passengers remained in her, though Ivor
Bentinck-Jones had seen fit to leave the ship at Athens, and
Jeremy Street had informed Nikki that he did not propose
to stay in her a day longer than his contract bound him to.

"When did you first suspect it was Ianthe?" Peter Trubody now asked. There were dark rings under his eyes, and
he presented a very much subdued appearance: he had
done a lot of growing up during the last few days—enough
to anticipate what was in Nigel's mind, for he added so-
berly, "You needn't mind—I shan't burst into tears or anything. It was only while I thought Melissa must have done
it—" He broke off, his lip trembling a little.

"First suspected Ianthe? Well, it didn't come in a blaze
of light, you know. I fancied it was Melissa for a while. It
had to be her or Ianthe, once the facts all pointed toward
the murder having been committed on Kalymnos. But
Melissa had no conceivable motive, whereas Ianthe had
two immensely strong ones."

"No, I mean the impersonation."

"Oh, it would be so much easier for Ianthe to pose as
Melissa than vice versa," Clare put in.

"Exactly. We all knew what Ianthe looked like—we'd

seen her face, always without make-up. None of us knew what Melissa looked like without it. Ianthe could make up to disguise herself as Melissa. If Melissa had been impersonating Ianthe, at the lecture on the boat deck, she'd have had to remove her make-up and the difference between their naked faces would be noticeable."

"But Ianthe couldn't have gone on the rest of her life posing as Melissa," said Peter. "She'd be bound to be shown up. I don't see what she expected to gain out of—out of the damnable things she did."

"That's just where you're wrong. But I'd better tell you her motives first, then what she planned to do, and then how it worked out in practice."

Nigel recounted what the Bishop of Solway had told him about the sisters' childhood—how Melissa had always been the favored one and their father could never show Ianthe true affection.

"Then Melissa married a rich man, who left her all his money when he died. Ianthe, though a brilliant scholar, was a failure as a schoolmistress; she'd recently been sacked, and might well fail to get another job. Also, she was a man-hater—or at least ill at ease with men—so she had little prospect of marriage. From childhood, she'd had good reason to envy her sister, to be jealous of her, to be poisoned with resentment and hatred."

"But Melissa would have given her money, supported her; she was immensely generous," Peter protested.

"I've no doubt she would. But imagine Ianthe forced to accept it—from Melissa of all people! Her pride and rancor simply wouldn't have tolerated charity from that source. Then she had this nervous breakdown. It crystallized all her resentment of her sister."

"Was she mad?" asked Faith. "She must have been."

"I don't think so. But the breakdown set her feet on the path toward murder. Melissa, whom she had not met for years, was cabled for. Melissa felt some guilt at having neglected her sister for so long; this cruise was part of her reparation. The two women had eyes of the same color and were of the same height and build. Ianthe would have seen Melissa without make-up, and realized that their faces were still very much alike, as they had been—so the Bishop told me—in childhood. He also told me that Ianthe had been a first-rate mimic then. I imagine the possibility of impersonating her sister entered Ianthe's mind first, in quite a vague way; then it spawned the idea of murdering her."

"But I just don't see it," Peter said. "How could she hope to pass herself off as Melissa for the rest of her life?"

"You must remember that Melissa was a rolling stone. After her husband died, she moved from place to place abroad, never staying anywhere long. All Ianthe would have to do would be to avoid the places where her restless sister had lived—and, of course, keep out of the way of Melissa's ex-lovers."

"Quite a job, that," Faith remarked.

"Oh, shut up!" said Peter. "Don't be so foul!"

Clare said, "But what about the money?"

"Melissa had no children. We shall find, probably, that she'd left all her money to Ianthe. But Ianthe was quite clever enough to realize that, if Melissa died by violence, she herself would be the first suspect, being sole heir. So she planned to—"

"No, I mean how would Ianthe, posing as Melissa, be able to get hold of the money?" asked Clare.

"Oh, easy. Typewritten letters to the brokers or solicitors or bank manager or whoever it might be; Melissa's signature forged; her account to be transferred to such-and-such a bank. But, mind you, she had been studying the part of Melissa very carefully. Melissa told me, on Delos, that, although Ianthe had previously shown no interest in her life for years, she had recently spent hours asking about her marriage, her travels, her friends, and so on. Ianthe was briefing herself, just in case she should run into someone who had known her sister."

"Ah, and that's why Ianthe did the watchdog act during the cruise," said Clare.

"Yes. We all noticed how she clung to Melissa. She could not risk anyone being alone with her sister for long, lest things might be said in conversation which Ianthe wouldn't know about when the time came for her to play the part of Melissa. And there was always a danger that Melissa would tell somebody that her sister had learned to swim when she was a child. We put it down to possessiveness on Ianthe's part. But, as Melissa told me, Ianthe had always been an independent, unclinging type before. One can imagine her jumping at the idea of a cruise; for with any luck no intimate of Melissa or herself would be on board, and if it became necessary to identify her sister's body, she'd be the only person competent to do so."

"It was all premeditated, then?"

"Very much so. Mind you, I fancy the outline of the crime appeared to her first as a fantasy—the way it does to intellectuals; she toyed with it, elaborated it, brooded over it, until she was possessed by it. No doubt, before they came to Greece, she'd been secretly practicing Melissa's signature, her style of make-up, her vocal intonations, and so on. And she must have decided early on that the method of murder should be drowning; from the start of the cruise she let it be known that she couldn't swim—a non-swimmer would not be suspected of drowning the victim. Whether the limp was originally part of the scheme or a brilliant last-minute improvisation, I don't know."

"But surely," said Peter, "it was an accident? Hurrying along that rough track to catch the steamer—"

"Oh no. It was absolutely necessary to the impersonation. Just to think."

"Necessary? I don't see it."

Clare said, "I think I do. She could mimic Melissa's voice, and make-up to look exactly like her—I suppose, by the way, she got herself the same hair-do as Melissa before they left England. But Melissa was a graceful woman, and Ianthe had a rather ungainly gait—"

"Exactly! The thing most likely to give you away, if you are trying to disguise yourself, is your walk. But Melissa limping would look no different from Ianthe limping. That's why I got so inquisitive about the turned ankle. It wasn't a fake. She did it quite deliberately."

"I think it's horrible," Faith exclaimed. "All the time she was sitting about on deck chairs, huddled up like a—like a basilisk, she was plotting how to do this dreadful thing."

"Yes. She was waiting for the right time and place, learning the layout of the ship, and above all presenting a picture of a woman imperfectly recovered from a nervous breakdown, ripe for suicide. I'll come back to that presently. Two things, though, she could not have foreseen— that you would be on board, Faith, and that Clare and I would. You and Peter were a great nuisance to her with your persecution campaign—"

"I'm sorry about that Aqua-Lung business," said Peter shamefacedly. "It was rather a silly trick, I suppose."

"Actually, I put him up to it," Faith confessed.

"You did, did you?" said Clare a little tartly. "Children, I was always told, shouldn't play with fire."

"I hated her. If only you knew how foully she behaved to me at school!"

"Oh, forget it, Faith!" Peter said. "It's over and done with. You talk as if she'd ruined you for life."

"Then there was Clare, with her trained eye, who saw the skull beneath the skin—the close similarity of bone structure. And there was me, with my trained mind and my professional inquisitiveness. Ianthe made one frightful gaffe, when she picked me to practice on."

"Practice on? What do you mean?"

"Clare and I were promenading the deck one night, and she called out to us, using Melissa's voice. We both thought it was Melissa, till we went up to her. I remembered that later. Well, the cove at Kalymnos gave Ianthe the chance she had been waiting for. She was a very clever woman, you realize, as well as a ruthless one. Her general scheme wasn't nearly so reckless as you might think. She would drown Melissa, change clothes with her, return alone to the ship as Melissa, hand in both landing cards together, say her sister had felt poorly and returned before her; after dinner, she would go to the cabin, remove make-up, put on her own clothes, attend the lecture, give an impression of acute melancholia, leave the lecture early, return to the cabin, and finally emerge as Melissa again. The disappearance of 'Ianthe' would be accepted quite naturally as suicide. If the body were found at all, it would not be found, in that unfrequented cove, for days or weeks, and the authorities would assume she had drifted back to the island after throwing herself off the ship. If the body were to be discovered before the cruise was over, Ianthe, posing as Melissa, was the person the authorities would send for to identify it. There was little likelihood of an investigation, under the circumstances. If the body were not discovered for some time, it would be unrecognizable anyway. But Ianthe had still worried about the possibility of distinguishing marks being noticed on Melissa's body. She tried to prevent her sister sunbathing in public. On the beach at Patmos she ticked Melissa off for not putting on a bathrobe over her bikini; I thought at the time it was just Ianthe's prudishness. Oh yes, and it was on this beach that I observed for the first time what Melissa kept in that wicker case she carried about everywhere."

"Her landing ticket, you mean?" asked Faith.

"Yes. But something else—her make-up materials. You see the point?"

"Well, no, I don't think I do."

"The dawn will come. Well, there we have Ianthe's outline plan. She would kill Melissa, become Melissa, and live on Melissa's income, happy forever after. And then the two sisters went to that desolate cove on Kalymnos, and Ianthe had the time, the place, and the unloved one, all together. We now come," said Nigel with a questioning glance at Peter, "to a pretty grim passage."

"It's all right. I can—I want to know," said Peter; but his lips had gone white.

"After Ianthe had got rid of the Chalmerses, both the sisters sunbathed. Posing as Melissa, Ianthe told me that she had gone to sleep for a bit. The real Melissa probably did—face down, on that flat rock, with little or nothing on. Ianthe, I suspect, had taken off all her own clothes; we know she'd been sunbathing a lot the last few days, to get her skin, which was sallow anyway, the color of Melissa's; also, the *Menelaos* passengers being on the whole a gentlemanly and ladylike lot, if anyone did turn up they'd probably avert their eyes from two naked females. Well, Melissa is lying face down, asleep. Ianthe hits her a violent blow on the back of the head, stunning her. Melissa's dress is lying nearby, and gets some blood on it; that's my theory, anyway; Ianthe had to plunge it in the sea presently, to wash off the bloodstains. But first she begins to put her own clothes on Melissa's body. While she's doing this, she notices that the wicker case had got dislodged and is floating out to sea. She at once plunges in after it."

"Because Melissa's make-up was in it, and Ianthe had none of her own there?" said Clare.

"I think so. If she couldn't make up there and then, her whole plan would be wrecked. Well, Primrose saw a swimmer retrieving the case, and thought it must be Ianthe because she was not wearing the yellow bathing cap that Melissa always wore. When Ianthe scrambled ashore again, she put on Melissa's bathing cap and finished dressing the body. That was what she was doing when Peter saw her. She'd lifted the body up a bit to slip her jumper over the head, and she let the head fall back with a crack onto the rock."

"Just as if it was—was a dummy in a shop window," Peter muttered. "Oh God!"

"Yes. She was not one to respect the dead. And she had the devil's own luck. If Peter hadn't removed himself at this point, he'd have seen her drag the unconscious woman into the sea, and wedge her under that overhanging rock to drown. Then Ianthe washed the bloodstained dress and made up her face. Presently she moved to the other side of the cove, so that she could dry the dress in the sun. Ianthe, as Melissa, returns to the ship. All goes well for a while. But then Primrose and Nikki between them contrive to complicate what had been a simple undertaking."

"Nikki? How?" asked Peter, with an undertone of jealousy in his voice.

"In a minute. Ianthe killed the wretched Primrose in the same way and for the same reason that I described when I was making a case against Melissa." Nigel outlined it for the benefit of the other two. He went on, "When she went out onto the fo'c's'le with Primrose, Ianthe suspected, from the way the child hinted at things, that she'd witnessed the murder of Melissa. Then Primrose pushed her into the swimming pool, and Ianthe lost her head and her temper, and dragged Primrose in and strangled her. It was her first bad mistake. With the child murdered, Ianthe's 'disappearance' could not be accepted so readily as the suicide of a deranged woman. Well, Ianthe managed to get back to the cabin. She took off her soaking clothes, and the next moment Nikki came prancing in. The cabin was dark—"

"You mean, Ianthe hadn't turned on the light? Why on earth not?" asked Clare.

"Panic. She'd only one thought in her head—to strip off the wet clothes which would betray her. It was a simple, instinctive compulsion to stay in the dark till she'd got a grip on herself again. But it was Nikki who got a grip on her. He thought it was the divine and willing Melissa. But the naked woman he found in the darkness there proved to be far from willing. She fought him savagely, *and in silence.* I ought to have seen the point of that long before I did."

"In silence?" Faith asked. "I don't get it."

"Melissa, if Peter will allow me, was a highly experienced woman. In fact, a bit of a whore. If the woman in the cabin had been Melissa, she'd never have been panicked by Nikki, never have fought; she'd have spoken to him, calmed him down, made some excuse for not wanting him just then. Or she might have let him have his way. But the woman in the cabin acted like an inexperienced virgin. She struggled. She dared not cry out, because it might bring other passengers into the cabin, who would turn on the light and see that it was Ianthe there. Even if it didn't, Nikki might have recognized that the voice was not Melissa's, for Ianthe was so agitated by what was happening that she knew she wouldn't be able to mimic Melissa's voice successfully. Well, she did get rid of Nikki. She dressed for the dance in Melissa's clothes, sprayed oil on her wet hair, and made up. She tended to overdo this, by the way. Mrs. Hale had remarked to me before the dance, at dinner, that Melissa was made up more heavily even than usual. But that was Ianthe's trouble. She overdid things. Like those swans."

"*Swans?* What swans?" said Faith, gaping at him.

"Ianthe behaved in a remarkably rational way, almost throughout," said Nigel, as if he had not heard the question. "She was a formidably intelligent woman, of course. She never attempted to cast suspicion on anyone else, for instance; and she stuck to her original plan, even after Primrose had pushed in and greatly complicated things. When I talked to her alone, the morning after the murders, she resisted the temptation to say too much."

"Did you know, then, that she was really Ianthe?" Peter asked.

"I knew the woman I was talking to must be Ianthe, unless I had misinterpreted every single piece of evidence. But I must admit there were moments when I could hardly believe she was not the real Melissa. She had Melissa's voice, and eyes, and pose. The features were somehow, indefinably, coarser; but that could have been the effect of shock and grief. And she did talk rather more intelligently than I'd heard Melissa talking. But on the whole she gave a wonderfully convincing impression of Melissa's personality."

"I'm not surprised," said Clare. "She'd always been jealous of her sister. As a girl, she'd desperately wanted to *be* Melissa—the daughter whom their father loved. I've no doubt, in those days, she copied Melissa often—consciously and unconsciously."

"Yes, that's a good point. The only time she seemed at all disconcerted, during this interview, was when I brought up the question of the wet dress. She couldn't help remembering the bloodstains she'd washed off. However, she recovered her poise very quickly, and gave me a natural explanation for its having got wet. No, she came through it extremely well, apart from her tendency to overdo things."

"Like those mysterious swans again, I suppose?" said Faith with an impish look.

Nigel again ignored the question. "Melissa was a fairly tough number. She admitted to me she was a selfish woman. Now I don't think Melissa would ever have been so shocked and prostrated by her sister's death—after all, Ianthe had threatened suicide—as the bogus Melissa gave herself out to be."

"She would have been, if she'd committed the murders."

"Certainly, Peter. But there was never any conceivable reason why Melissa should kill Ianthe. But if it was the other way around, as I believed it was, Ianthe would need all the respite and privacy she could get; so the bogus Melissa exaggerated the natural effects of shock. If I hadn't been there to poke my nose in, I believe she'd still have got away with it, in spite of the Primrose complication."

"If the Greek police are as susceptible as Nikki, she would," Clare said.

"They'd not have pressed her hard. With any luck, she could rely on their accepting the theory that Ianthe had had a brainstorm, murdered Primrose, and then thrown herself off the ship. Ianthe had been playing up her nervous condition like mad for days, and—"

"Like the swans?" said Faith.

"What *is* all this about swans?" Peter demanded.

"I can tell you," said Clare dreamily. "They had ants in their wing-pits."

"Which of course explains everything," Peter dryly remarked.

"It does, you know," said Nigel. "From the start of the

voyage, I was puzzled by Ianthe's behavior. She jumped out of her skin whenever the ship's siren blew. She sat about the deck, looking like a lump of dough sodden with misery. She twitched and winced and flared up. She made a scene at Jeremy Street's first lecture. She made a scene in the cave on Patmos; and she made yet another when I offered my sympathy over this. She was deliberately building up the impression of an unstable mind. Now, if she'd genuinely been as bad as all that, the doctors would never have allowed her out of the nursing home. Melissa told me, that day on Delos—"

"What a lot Melissa told you that day on Delos," Clare remarked.

"Yes. She told me the doctors had said it was quite all right for Ianthe to go on a cruise; she was 'well over the worst.' But Ianthe was now telling Melissa she had nothing worth living for, couldn't go on any longer, etc. So I began to wonder, quite idly, what all this malingering was in aid of. Why should Ianthe give these public exhibitions of a suicidal tendency? But I dare say my mind would never have started working on this line, but for something that happened months before the cruise."

"Ah, now we come to them at last," said Faith.

"Yes. Clare and I were walking by the Serpentine, and we saw a mob of swans behaving in a very peculiar way." Nigel described the scene in detail. "So Clare made some frivolous and heartless remark about their being afflicted with ants."

"And you said they must be having a nervous breakdown," Clare put in.

"And what did *you* say then, my love?"

"I can't recollect. Something forceful and intelligent, I've no doubt."

"It was. More so than you knew. You said, 'Well, if they are, they're overdoing it badly.' "